DETROIT PUBLIC LIBRARY

P9-DNO-451

Chase Branch Library
17731 W. Seven Mile Rd.
Detroit, MI 48235

SEP - - 2015

CH

A SCHOOL OF Dolls

A NOVEL

PAIGE LOHAN

By Paige Lohan

A<u>RE</u> Y<u>OU</u> O<u>N</u> O<u>UR</u> E<u>MAIL</u> L<u>IST</u>?

S<u>IGN UP ON OUR WEBSITE</u>

<u>www.thecartelpublications.com</u>

<u>OR TEXT THE WORD: CARTELBOOKS</u>

T<u>O</u> <u>22828</u>

<u>FOR PRIZES, CONTESTS, ETC.</u>

CHECK OUT OTHER TITLES BY THE CARTEL PUBLICATIONS

By Paige Lohan

WWW.THECARTELPUBLICATIONS.COM

A SCHOOL OF DOLLS

BY

Paige Lohan

A School of Dolls   7

Copyright © 2015 by The Cartel Publications. All rights
reserved.
No part of this book may be reproduced in any form
without permission
from the author, except by reviewer who may quote
passages
to be printed in a newspaper or magazine.

PUBLISHER'S NOTE:
This book is a work of fiction. Names, characters,
businesses,
Organizations, places, events and incidents are the
product of the
Author's imagination or are used fictionally. Any
resemblance of
Actual persons, living or dead, events, or locales are
entirely coincidental.

Library of Congress Control Number: 2015950380

ISBN 10: 0989084566

ISBN 13: 978-0989084567

Cover Design: Davida Baldwin www.oddballdsgn.com
www.thecartelpublications.com
First Edition
Printed in the United States of America

By Paige Lohan

What's Up Fam,

I hope your summer wasn't too fast and you had the chance to enjoy it with your loved ones. This summer was a tough one for me, but I am tremendously blessed and refuse to complain, so moving on.

A School of Dolls is finally up at bat. I truly enjoyed it and found myself laughing out loud and shaking my head at some of the predicaments Paige had her characters in. I'm sure you will like it too.

With that being said, keeping in line with tradition, we want to give respect to a vet or trailblazer paving the way. In this novel, we would like to recognize:

Lauren Francis-Sharma

Lauren Francis-Sharma is the author of the novel, *'Til The Well Runs Dry*. It is a very captivating tale of love of family and scandal set in Trinidad in the 1940s and 1960s. The Caribbean serves as the perfect canvas to paint the author's story during this time. Make sure you check it out, but be warned; you will probably be in the mood for some Jamaican or Caribbean food while you're reading it, so enjoy!

Aight, get to it. I'll catch you in the next novel.

Be Easy!

Charisse "C. Wash" Washington

Vice President

The Cartel Publications

www.thecartelpublications.com

www.facebook.com/publishercwash

Instagram: publishercwash

www.twitter.com/cartelbooks

www.facebook.com/cartelpublications

Follow us on Instagram: Cartelpublications

#CartelPublications

#UrbanFiction

#PrayForCeCe

#PrayForSeven

By Paige Lohan

#ASchoolOfDolls

PROLOGUE

NORTH CAROLINA

*T*he cafeteria, slightly dark and cool, smelled of twenty-three teenage football players after a hot sweaty game. Each of them had their sights on two victims who wondered where the anger originated.

The schoolmates they trusted — whom they washed dirty uniforms for and cleaned up after in the locker room, surrounded the scared classmates like predators.

Joe and Luke, cousins, watched the mob close in on them after having been stripped of their clothing. It was certain that they feared for their lives. Trembling, they stood arm and arm, wondering what would happen next.

Marcus Johnson, the quarterback stepped from the pack and looked at Joe Pell first. The athlete's face was contorted with anger and the cousins could feel the rage steaming from his pores. Without warning he raised his hand and smacked Joe with thunder, causing him to buckle and fall to his knees.

"Why did you make me chase you?" he asked cracking his knuckles. "And then why come here? Don't you two faggies realize we gotta eat in this bitch?" he paused. "Must you contaminate everything you touch?"

12   By Paige Lohan

As Joe wept quietly from the floor, large streams of tears rolled down his cousin Luke's blushed butter colored cheeks as he awaited his fate. Knowing it was coming he braced himself as best as he could by tensing his body and closing his eyes tightly.

Although savagery was in the air at the moment the day started simple enough. The South Carolina Banshees went on to play the North Carolina Bobcats in a rival football match that they clearly were unprepared for. Not even fifteen minutes into the game Marcus, quarterback of the Bobcats, was sacked three times resulting in a shameful landslide loss.

After the defeat, filled with anger the Bobcats piled into the locker room, only to see Joe and Luke dancing to "Drunk In Love" by Beyoncé. Hips swaying back and forth, they moved like women, which at the moment irritated Marcus to no end. It wasn't as if the team was unaware that their peers were gay, it's just that the recent loss had them feeling resentful, due to stealing their chances at a championship run. As far as Marcus was concerned who better to take it out on then two gay boys who were defenseless standing next to Marcus' 6'4 inch height and muscular arms?

Storming toward them Marcus snapped.

He walked up to the radio, tossed it across the way and slammed a fist into the locker causing both of them to tremble. The music no longer played in the background. "I'm sick of you niggas coming in here with this gay shit!" The team, also looking to get off a little steam, circled the duo. "Somebody got to remind you dudes that you ain't bitches." His gaze swiveled between them. "Take off your fucking clothes!"

A large hush grew over the locker room, the teammates wondering where their captain was going.

Joe smiled uneasily, his light honey colored skin-producing puddles of sweat along his hairline. "Stop playing," Joe said jokingly. "We were just fucking around, if you want us gone we can bounce."

"Yeah, Marcus," Luke replied with a larger grin, trying to appear more confident than his cousin that all would be okay. "Why you so serious when you know we be just playing?"

Marcus stepped closer, his teeth bearing. It was apparent that he wasn't in the mood.

"I...said...take...your...fucking...clothes...off!"

Although the team had no understanding of why Marcus would request two admitted gay classmates to undress, they knew better than to challenge him.

Realizing he had to do what he was told, first Joe removed his sweaty white t-shirt, followed by his jean shorts.

By Paige Lohan

"The underwear too," Marcus coached, pointing at them.

Reluctantly Joe complied, cupping his hands in front of his penis when he stood amongst them naked. Luke now receiving the brunt of Marcus' evil attention because he was still clothed, quickly hopped out of his blue jeans and red t-shirt.

Marcus smiled and looked back at his teammates deviously, who were happy he hadn't gone totally mad, because at least he acknowledged them. "Look at these scrawny ass niggas! If I hit either one of them they'd break!"

"Can we leave now?" Joe asked. "We won't bother you — "

Marcus pressed his massive hand on the right side of Joe's head and slammed it against the locker so hard he temporarily loss hearing in his left ear. Blood splashed everywhere and when he regained his balance he and Luke went running out of the locker room, in the nude, for their lives. Not being done with them, Marcus and his teammates took off in a violent pursuit.

Unfortunately for the cousins they arrived at a dead end, the chained up school cafeteria. Basically help could not come in from the outside.

With nowhere else to go they had a feeling the worse had yet to come.

Standing next to the table Marcus said, "Now say you're sorry for faking like girls when you niggas." He looked into Luke's eyes. "Tell me you nothing but the pathetic freaks that I know you to be. And beg me not to kill you."

"I'm nothing but the – " Luke's sentence was severed when Marcus socked him in the mouth so hard his jaw relocated to one side of his face. Marcus' fellow teammates showed zero sympathy as they cheered their quarterback on, wondering what act of brutality he would perform next.

"Get up!" he demanded both of them who were on the cool ground.

Having been struck first, Joe covered his penis while Luke looked up from the floor in fear, refusing to rise to his feet.

"Fine, if you don't want to get up, we'll bring the heat down to you." He looked back at his men. "Finish these fuck boys off."

Instantly fists, kicks and shoves bombarded the cousins from all angles. There was no place to run and no place to hide. The only thing they could do was succumb to the pain.

And so they did.

16   By Paige Lohan

CHAPTER ONE

A YEAR LATER

JOE

I didn't want to be here...

All of the loud screams and cheers after the verdict was read made me feel like I was in a circus instead of a courtroom. But here I was, witnessing the school board being found guilty of neglect. And although we won our case, the only thing I wanted to do was get out of this building, put my mother in bed and lay next to her while she rubbed my hair.

I still can't believe all of this happened. Although we weren't really friends, before they jumped us, Marcus was cool. On the days they won, when the rest of the football team went home, he would kick it with me and Luke at the Dance Deli in the city. And whenever people would tease him about being gay for hanging with us he would get with them quick, and they always left us alone. But this day he was somebody different. Someone who seemed to hate us because of who we were.

When my mother first filed charges I didn't think we would win. It was hard being gay down south in the Bible belt, so Luke and me kept our lifestyle a secret. If it hadn't been for Luke's flaming gay personality we would have gotten away with it, or at least I think so.

To my surprise in the end the school was found negligent because after the football game was over the supervising adults remained outside on the field, giving interviews to a few local papers about the loss. And while they were out there answering questions from the press, we were almost killed inside.

"You did it, honey," my mother said as she touched my face with her cool hands. Her eyes appeared to go deeper into her face and her baldhead was covered with a blue silk scarf. Cancer was eating at her flesh, leaving very little of my mother behind. "I know it's been hard on you, on both of you, but now you can put it behind you and start your life over." She looked at me and my cousin who was sitting on the other side of me being rude.

When he didn't respond I looked over at Luke and saw his cell phone was in his hand and he was playing with a calculator. It was like none of the cameras and

By Paige Lohan

people trying to get at us bothered him. "My mama talking to you, what you doing?"

He looked at her and said, "Oh, I'm sorry, Aunt Poochy, I was just adding up all the trinkets I'm gonna buy with that million dollar judgment." He continued to stab in numbers. "I just wish we didn't have to wait until we were eighteen to get our coins."

I put my hand over his phone and said, "Stop playing around, plus we gotta get mama out of here." We both stood up and I looked around the courtroom, wondering how we would leave without microphones being pressed against our lips.

Although all of the media attention made me uncomfortable, I knew why it was big news. Because of the incident, I suffered a broken neck and a fractured right foot. Luke's hip was misplaced and his jaw was broken. And even though the football players were expelled, the city was divided. Most of them blamed Luke, and me especially after Marcus lied and said we came on to him, saying that's why they beat us. In the end our injuries were our faults and no one cared but my mama.

When I saw two security guards with angry glares coming toward us I said, "Come on, mama, we got to get out of here while we can." I helped her to her feet and with the help of the guard we pushed past the crowd and toward the car.

I was halfway out when I looked behind me and saw that Luke was gone. I could feel my skin getting heated because all he had to do was stay close, instead he was somewhere in the sea of people who looked like they wanted to hurt us more than get our part of the story.

Still holding my mother's hand I finally saw my cousin and I wished I hadn't. He was holding the mic along with the reporter, smiling and winking at the camera like he was a star. Although there were a lot of people talking I recognized his voice immediately over the crowd.

"Yes, um, I was scared, but as long as they pay me my money, I'm good, you feel me, girl?" he said waving his arms and flicking his wrists. Unlike me Luke was the epitome of gay, loud voice, flicking wrists and all.

He must've felt me staring at him because he stopped the interview in midsentence and caught up with me. "I'm sorry, cuz, the public couldn't wait."

"If my mama gets hurt we fighting," I told him as we continued to try to leave the large crowd.

We were almost free when a white man with pasty skin and red splotches stepped up to us. "I can't believe they gave you fags a million dollars because you suck dick! Instead of money you deserve to rot in hell! And if you ask me those boys did you a favor by trying to beat some sense into you."

My mother, who is barely able to stand without help, pushed away from me and spit in his face. A long glob of mucus hung off the end of his nose. "How dare you come in my face and talk to my son and nephew that way!" she pointed at him. "You don't know what they endured! They almost died! If I was stronger I would give you a taste of what they experienced." Her brows lowered. "Be lucky I'm not."

He wiped his nose off, rolled his eyes and stormed away.

When I looked around I noticed that the security guards who were supposed to protect us had gone. I'm not surprised, they looked like they didn't want to help us anyway. For a second the three of us stood in the middle of a sea of reporters, onlookers, supporters and haters. On one side were colorful rainbow flags waving in the air and on the other were signs that read, "God hates Fags".

I looked down at my mother; her cheeks red and huge tears rolling down her face. "This world is not safe for my boys," she said under her breath. "What am I going to do? How am I going to protect you?"

Luke and me were in front of the house trying to scrub the shit stains off the side of our home with thick yellow plastic gloves. Last night while we slept, some haters decided to leave human waste all on the side of our house. And to prevent my mother from seeing it, since she spent most of her days out on the porch, Luke and me got up early to clean up the mess, although he fought me about it every minute.

On days like this I wish my mother never agreed to let him stay with us two years ago. He was too ungrateful and lazy. It wasn't like we had money or even the space. Him living here meant I would have to share my room and sometimes the attention of my

By Paige Lohan

mother, but there was no way she was going to see him out on the street. Or any family member in need for that matter.

Let me go back a little.

My father, who was white, spent most of his life on a boat as a fisherman. The only thing he loved more than the sea was my mother and anybody who spent a minute around them could see their love. He met her when she was a cook for a large vessel that made millions a year. They both worked on the ship. They would be gone for months at a time and when the catch was over, they would head back home, and somehow they found time to fall in love.

After a few months of dating it wasn't long before she got pregnant and had me. She use to always say that the only thing Richard wanted her to do was raise a happy child and to leave the money making to him. So she gave up the lifestyle and relied on my father to pay the bills.

He did a good job too. My father made six figures even though all we wanted was his time. It seemed like he was never home, only staying a few weeks at a time and leaving for months. After awhile I knew it wasn't possible and that what he did for a living meant he had to be gone. In return he bought us the biggest house money could buy and there wasn't a day I can remember that I wasn't sporting designer labels when I went to school.

And then it happened, a storm the forecasters didn't predict or else my father would not have gone. Before he had a family he was the first one to brave the wild waters for the catch but after us he turned down any trip that could be dangerous. It didn't matter, he was already there and the hurricane waves washed over my father's boat, killing all fifty something people on board. The ocean swallowed the only man who ever loved me.

My mother was devastated after that, and it wasn't too much longer that she started complaining of not feeling well. Before my father died my mother was the picture of perfect health, and just like that everything changed. She grew sick and frail. I know for a fact that cancer can take you if your spirit is weak, my mother is living proof. Sometimes I think she wants to die.

Not even six months later my Aunt Stacy, on my father's side, lost her daughters, my cousins, in a car accident. To this day nobody knows exactly what

By Paige Lohan

happened, just that alcohol may have been involved and that my aunt was responsible.

I guess death wasn't done with us because a month after that my Aunt Sidney killed her husband Gregg, before turning the .45 handgun on herself. And that's when Luke moved in.

He always acted like nothing bothered him and even called my Aunt Sidney stupid for killing herself over a cheating nigga that happened to be his father. But I knew it ripped at him, which is why he stayed getting into trouble, sometimes bringing me with him.

"I can't believe this!" Luke said as he scrubbed hard poop off the steps. "People act like what happened to us was our fault!"

"It will soon be over," I said. "Right now lets just clean the house so mama can come out here and enjoy the sun, besides, I'm starting to really worry about her."

Luke sighed and dumped his sponge in a bucket of soapy water. "I noticed she seems to be getting weaker too. And it fucks me up that she has to go through all of this; this is why I hate this state! If everybody not moving the same, and believing in the same things, it's a problem."

A School of Dolls   25

"I really don't think we gonna have to go through this forever. Give it a few months, somebody else will be in the paper and they will forget all about us."

"There you go doing that weak shit again." He said angrily.

"What you talking about?"

"Being optimistic," he said throwing the sponge in the bucket, before tossing his gloves on the porch. "Sometimes it's okay to be mad, Joe. Sometimes it's okay to express how you feel about things. You don't always have to take the high road because for real it makes you seem fake."

"How do you know I'm not expressing how I feel?"

"Because you're too lax with your attitude. Them niggas broke your neck, my hip and my jaw. I don't even walk the same and I doubt I ever will. And now we're cleaning their shit up? The last thing I feel like being right now is diplomatic when I want to be mad."

"So what you gonna do about it? Be mean to everybody?"

"Sometimes I think about getting a gun, walking up to Marcus and blowing his brains out."

My jaw hung because I didn't expect that. "Excuse me?"

"Let's just say you handle things the way you do, and I'll handle things my way. Cool?"

"Boys, come here," I heard my mother yell from inside of the house.

Hearing her voice we ran inside washed our hands and walked to her bedroom. I sat on the edge of her bed and tried to catch my breath due to the heat. Mama's room always felt like hell but she liked it that way, saying cool air troubled her bones. Touching her hand I said, "Something wrong?"

She looked at me, smiled and gazed at Luke. "I talked to your Aunt Stacy today, and she's agreed to do what I asked, and I know you don't like it but trust me when I say it's for the best."

I removed my hand from hers and covered my face. "Mama, why did you do that?" I sighed. "I don't want to live with her, plus you know how she is. I want to be here with you while you're sick."

"Me too Aunt Poochy. You need us here and we can't be that going all the way to Baltimore

Maryland. What happens if you need help and can't get it?"

"Let me worry about that, all I know is that it's not safe for you here. Until things die down it's important that I do all I can to give you some semblance of life. Some safety. And we can't do that when every time you walk out the door someone throws something at you or yells about how you're going to burn in hell." She coughed and took a few moments to regain her composure. "I'm sorry, but I can't play when it comes to your lives anymore. You both will have to leave, and that's final."

"But who's gonna take care of you, ma?" I pleaded. "Who's gonna make sure you got everything you need?"

"I've contacted someone at the Cancer Center and they're going to dispatch a nurse to help me with my day-to-day functions. During the weekends a few friends have already agreed to stop by, but I really don't want you boys to worry."

"Mama, I hate this," I said with tears streaming down my face.

"I know, son, which is why I'm asking you to do this for me." She paused. "Because if someone else hurts you, I'm gonna take what's left of my life and commit murder. Is that what you want?"

CHAPTER TWO

BALTIMORE, MD

LUKE

I had to admit when I first got the 'T' that we were moving in with Aunt Stacy I had a problem, that was before I forgot she was rich. She had come into some money when her daughters died in a car accident some years back, and as much as she hit the bottle I would've thought the cash would be gone by now.

But looking at how laid out things were I'm elated I was wrong.

Sitting on the edge of my pink twin bed, with the matching color scheme throughout the room, I was surprised at how much thought Aunt Stacy put into making me comfortable. Even Joe, who rarely liked a thing, thought the teal green color scheme in his room was nice.

For me it was more special because I'm not related to Aunt Stacy. She's Joe's father's sister so she didn't have to let me move in, but I fucked with her. As I walked around the room, the smell of newness around

By Paige Lohan

me, there was one thing on my mind, what did she *really* want?

The last time I saw Aunt Stacy she was sitting on our toilet, with her clothes on pissing into her jeans. I hated when she came over Aunt Poochy's because when she hit the bottle she forced everyone else to have to take care of her. One time she even got so ripped at a club she lost her pants and sat ass naked on the ground, legs spread wide, as she showed a few hookers what she thought was a cute pussy.

That day was a nightmare. At first I thought somebody died when a friend of Aunt Poochy's called early in the morning to come get her sister-in-law. Since Aunt Poochy was sick, Joe and me had to ride with her to pick Stacy up. The next morning she was up cooking breakfast, wondering why everyone in the house was mad at her.

Chile, she had forgotten everything.

When my door opened my cousin Joe came inside. His features were so feminine that I often wondered when he would realize he could be a model, but he always waved me off. In Joe's mind he was too good for a career that judged a person based on their looks. He had aspirations of moving to L.A. or New York, where he could become a magician. Bye girl...so stupid! Pulling cards from behind people's ears may be cute at seventeen, but I doubt very seriously he'll get the same reception as an old queen in his forties.

"So you like it?" He asked walking around my room. As his eyes roamed I could tell he was looking for something to be judgmental about. Not surprising. He's such a hater.

"I love it actually, what about you? Or let me guess, the bed is too big and the curtains are too pretty."

He laughed. "To be honest the only complaint I got is that I don't want to be here." He shrugged. "The idea of mama being in North Carolina by herself makes me uncomfortable."

"She gonna be fine, baby." I waved the air.

"It's easy for you to say, your mother not here no more."

The moment he said that I felt like scratching his eyes out. All my life my cousin has low key hated me, whether he admits it or not. He threw shade because of the relationship I have with his mother, believing we spend too much time together. Our bond wasn't out of malice. Aunt Poochy just happens to like older music, and so do I. I can listen to some of the

By Paige Lohan

stuff out today but for real my flavor is Patti Labelle, Smokey Robinson and musicians like that. So naturally we would get along better because he's a trap queen.

He's also jealous because before I came to his high school he was rolling around with the weak crowd. It was me who breathed some popularity into his dying social life but he claimed I was doing too much to fit in. I might not have a body like Joe but when it comes to the personality he has nothing on me, which his why he stayed tossing stones.

"I didn't mean it like that, Luke, I just want to be home that's all."

"Then go back home! Why stay here if you feel like you hate it so much? As far as I know you agreed to come, but I'm sure it can be arranged for you to leave. All you have to do is tell your aunt."

He wrapped his arms around his body and sighed. He gazed out of my window. "I think Aunt Stacy just pulled up." I can tell he wanted to skip the subject and as long as I got my point across I was okay with it.

"She back from the store already?" I walked over to the dresser, picked up a brush and stroked my short hair. As I ran the brush over my scalp I imagined I had a long lustrous mane and that my boyfriend was behind me, whispering in my ear. Most days I feel like a girl trapped in a boy's body and it kills me some times.

"I think so," he sighed again and I wanted him to stop. No matter where we were I got the impression that he wanted to be some place else. "You really think all of this is a good idea? Knowing how she is?"

"I don't think we have a choice," I shrugged. "Your mother was clear, we had to leave so we did."

A few minutes later Aunt Stacy came into the room, holding a brown paper bag. She was wobbling a little and I knew immediately that whatever she was drinking wasn't sweet tea. "Did your mama tell you what I said on the phone today?" she asked looking at Joe and then me. "I think she thought I was playing but I'm dead serious."

"She's my aunt," I reminded her. "Not my mother."

Her eyes widened as if she just remembered. "I'm sorry, Luke, she had you for so long I almost forgot."

Well I didn't.

"What did you want her to tell us?" Joe asked, stuffing his hands into his pockets. He seemed worried, probably thinking something happened to Aunt Poochy.

"First let me say that she wasn't too pleased about my plan, but I have an idea that will help you both get through school unharmed. Now before you say anything understand that I thought about this for a very long time. To me there's no better way, and I'm actually pretty sure you'll like my idea."

Joe moved closer. "I'm confused."

She cleared her throat, removed the top off of the bottle and took a large gulp. "To prevent what happened in North Carolina, from happening here, I think you should become girls." She looked at us, her head nodding with drunkenness. "Well, not girls in the traditional sense, obviously you'll still have your dicks, but girls none the less. You're both so pretty I know you can pull it off."

I broke out laughing and walked closer. Figuring she was telling a joke I waited for the punch line but it never came. "Auntie, you're playing right?"

She focused on me as best as she could and said, "Not even close."

"How and why would we do something like that?" Joe asked.

"You were just involved in one of the biggest cases of hate crime of the century. Now there are people, even in Baltimore, who have a problem with how the verdict went down. Those same people want to see to it that you feel their frustration. But if you're girls, if you change your name and identities, you have a chance at a second life. Nobody will know who you are. This way your mother doesn't have to worry about you. And I won't have to worry either."

About once a month, in the small town we lived in I would secretly dress in drag. I would go through Aunt Poochy's closet, pick out the best from the worst, and go out to McDonald's or some place short to get attention. When I grabbed one of her wigs and did my makeup, nobody *ever*, suspected me of being anything other than a girl. So quite honestly I had no problem with Aunt Stacy's request. I thought it was original. "If you think it's for the best, I'm here for it," I responded, probably a tad too quickly.

"You sound stupid," Joe said, his eyes dark as he stared at me.

I turned toward him. "Why is it stupid? People out there in the world hate us, Joe. They don't want us to live our lives and if we have a chance to start all over

By Paige Lohan

and finish high school without a major production starring us then I'm here for that. You should be too."

Joe paced my room and leaned up against the dresser before looking at Aunt Stacy. "I don't get it, why would you try and make us out to be liars?"

"All I want is you to live," she said softly. "It ain't like you have more than a year left in school, sweetheart. Be smart about this."

Joe stood up straight, dropping his hands at his sides. "If this is the only way then I won't do it. I rather deal with whatever in North Carolina."

"Joe!" I yelled.

He waved me off. "I'm not going to deny who I am just so that some people who don't know nothing about me can feel comfortable. It took me too long to get out of the closet, I'm not going back in by dressing like a girl."

"I think you're making a big mistake," Aunt Stacy pleaded, moving a little closer to him.

"This from a woman who can't handle her own fucking liquor." He stomped out, slamming the bedroom door behind himself.

CHAPTER THREE

JOE

I called my mother and told her I couldn't do my Aunt Stacy and she wasn't happy about it. It was the first time I heard her yell at me and I didn't want to hear it again. After she calmed down I asked if she told her what she wanted us to do and she seemed clueless. I think the medicine she's taking messes up her mind.

"Not sure what she has planned for you boys, and if she told me I can't remember," she said, with her voice sounding weaker. "The medicine they have me on drains me so badly. But I do know her house is the best place for you at this time, and I really wish you could play fair with her, Joe. Meet her half way because she really cares about you."

I heard what she was saying but my mind was made up. I didn't want to be with anybody who didn't want me to be myself. We were on the phone for fifteen minutes before I convinced her that I really needed to come back. "If it bothers you that bad I'll pay for a ticket for you to come home, although I really believe this is a mistake. People don't just want to hurt you here, they want to kill you."

"I'll be careful, mama, I just can't take it here anymore."

I didn't bother telling her about me and Luke being in drag because as long as I didn't have to do it, I saw no need in making her feel worse by learning that Aunt Stacy was not the person that she claimed to be.

My plan was to go to my aunt's house, pack my things and leave on the first flight going back to North Carolina in the morning.

Wanting a little air, and not being ready to go home, I sat at the bus stop to go nowhere. My aunt's weird suggestion and Luke's too happy face when he heard it played in my mind repeatedly.

After the bus came, I got on and dosed off. I guess I was more tired than I realized. I hopped off when I woke up and saw a burger shack that seemed to be a little empty. Once inside I ordered a cheeseburger, fries and a strawberry shake and sat in the corner of the restaurant.

I was halfway done with my meal when I saw a group of black kids about my age looking in my direction. At first I didn't think anything of the stares because I've gotten some really nice compliments in the past. Everything from the mole on my right cheek was cute to I'm so pretty I could be a girl.

But when the kids looking at me talked in a huddle while gazing my way, I figured something else was going on. After a few minutes one of them stomped up to me, his face wrinkled because he was frowning so hard. "Fuck you looking at, faggy?"

I dropped my head and played around with one of the fries. I had never been a fighter and I didn't want to start today. All I wanted was to finish my food and go home, and if I had to I was willing to leave my meal if I could leave unharmed.

"I asked you a question, bitch," he said before knocking my food off the table.

My heartbeat kicked up and I suddenly felt feverish. What was I supposed to say behind his question? My words evaporated every time I opened my mouth and I found myself silent.

I was about to say I had no problem with him until I saw he reached into the crease of his pocket. Not knowing what he was about to do I stood up, grabbed my cup and tossed what was left of my shake in his face. I took off running, his screams behind me as I ran outside for my life.

When I turned around all of them were behind me and my teeth knocked against one another, my entire body trembling. I don't think I can take another dose of what happened to me in Carolina, and it looked like that was about to go down all over again.

I was almost away from them until I ran into the middle of the street, right in front of oncoming traffic.

I was standing on the side of my bed looking down at all of the clothes Aunt Stacy pulled out. I think she got these from her daughters but they still looked new. There were tight jeans; dresses and full lace wigs that you could part anywhere and it would look like a natural scalp. Although everything was stylish I wondered why first, she was so hospitable and second, why this was so important to her. She said it was because she loved us but to me there was more.

After checking out all of the outfits I looked at my face in the mirror. I hadn't been in Baltimore 24 hours before I suffered another black eye. It seemed that no matter how hard I tried to get away from the past, someone was waiting to bring me down. For months my face was plastered all over television and people acted out their hate for gay people on me. Had it not been for the undercover police officer whose car I ran in front of after I caught a fist from the bully, I would probably be dead.

He wasted no time running the gang of boys off and helping me to my feet. He also recognized who I was. "You that kid on television right? The one who just won the millions?"

I nodded yes, and swallowed the lump in my throat.

"I knew I recognize your face," he said excitedly before growing a little calmer. "Listen, I don't know who your parents are but I can tell you this, a lot of people thought them boys were justified for what they did to you."

"It was my fault I was beat almost to death?"

"Not saying that. What I am saying is that maybe you should stay incognito. You know, do all

By Paige Lohan

you can to stay off the radar. People like me won't always be there to protect you." After that he walked away.

As I caught the bus back to my aunt's, eyeball throbbing. I knew he was right. Until everything blew over I need to do what was best for me even if that meant becoming a girl. And I was willing to do anything if it meant I could finish school, wait for the check to clear on our settlement and maybe move my mother somewhere away from it all.

I was still in the mirror when I heard Aunt Stacy yell, "Boys, please come here. I want to talk to you for a minute."

I put the last of my clothes in my closet and walked to the living room. She was sitting on the sofa wearing a two-piece red camese and large underwear that managed to ride deeply into the walls of her pale white thighs. "Yes, Auntie?" I tried not to look at her but it was sad. She did all she could for attention, even if it was from us.

"Do you like your things?" she asked looking at Luke and then at me.

"Yes," I smiled sitting on the recliner away from her. "I can't believe you did all of that. I mean the wigs." I knew the clothes were old.

"If we're going to do this it's important that I see the thing through." She smiled. "But we have to get on the same page in order for this to work."

"Sure, Auntie," Luke said. "What gives?"

"Tomorrow you'll have school and I know you may be excited but it's important that you get used to answering by the names you've chosen. Until school is over you are no longer Joe or Luke, so I don't want you calling yourselves those names in the house." She looked at me. "Okay, Joanne?"

I nodded, still uncomfortable with it all.

"Are you in agreement, Lolita?" She looked at Luke.

Excitedly he said, "Of course!"

I'm not gonna lie, his perkiness about everything made me angry. Why didn't he see the danger in this as much as I did? Why was it so easy for him to pretend to be something he wasn't while it was eating me inside?

"Perfect!" she clapped her hands together while her thighs jiggled. "This is going to work and if we do it right it can be enjoyable too."

"Enjoyable?" I said sarcastically. "Because we get to wear dresses and wigs?"

"Not just that, Joanne. I figured you would love being openly feminine. I mean you are gay right?"

"Just because I'm gay doesn't mean I want to dress like a girl."

"I wish you wouldn't take things so literally," Luke said. "She just wanted us to have a little fun."

"Well I'm not in the mood for fun."

Luke rolled his eyes and I did the same.

Aunt Stacy sighed. "Maybe enjoyable was the wrong word, I just want you to make the best of it." She crossed her arms over her body before dropping them at her sides. "A few more things, I don't want you to ever spend more than a couple of hours over a friend's house. The longer you're there, the more easily it is for those around you to discover your secret. You have to always be on guard because you never know when you may slip up. Also if you happen to visit a friend, never use the bathroom."

Frowning I asked, "Why not?"

"Because you can never risk someone walking in or you forget to put the seat down." She paused. "I just want you both to be as careful as possible. Mess up in the slightest and this could go very badly."

"They won't catch me slipping, honey." Luke bragged. "I'm too smooth for that shit."

"Yeah, you do a real good job of lying," I said.

"Hater," he winked.

This bitch is making me mad.

"I'm serious, girls," she said angering me even more. "We are going to have to play this out perfectly. So, on second thought for friends, if you choose to keep time with folks, I prefer if you bring them here. Everything in this house is geared around keeping your secret. I've placed everything about you both being boys in the basement and locked the door, so that you never have to worry about being caught if your friends come over. So consider this your safe zone."

"Sounds like you have it all under control," I said.

"I do, but there's one more thing. You can never, ever, have boyfriends. It's too risky. Remember the reason why we're doing this...to prevent you both from having to deal with what you've dealt with in the past, and a boyfriend contradicts that." She looked at both of us. "Am I clear?"

I cleared my throat. To be honest I hadn't thought about being with any boys but the fact that I couldn't if I was interested was annoying.

"I get it, auntie," Luke said.

"Me too."

She clapped her hands together again. "Good, now go and put on one of the outfits and wigs. I want to see how you look."

I stomped toward my room. When I got inside I placed a form fitting black dress on along with my jean jacket and Uggs. Then I grabbed my black full lace wig and looked at myself in the mirror. Even without the makeup I looked...pretty.

Taking a big breath I walked into the living room and saw Luke who was wearing a pair of tight jeans and a white top. If I didn't know it was my cousin I would've said, "She's fierce." His curves are not like mine but his face makes being a girl real believable.

I was so caught up with him that I didn't see Aunt Stacy staring at us. Her pale skin blushed a little and she seemed beyond excited. Closing her hanging mouth she said, "Oh my, goodness, you look as beautiful as dolls."

By Paige Lohan

CHAPTER FOUR

LUKE

I have never felt more like myself then I do today.

When I glanced over at Joe, now Joanne, as we walked toward the entrance of Daniel Day High School I couldn't get over how pretty he looked. We both elected to wear jeans to tone our appearance down, although I finished my fit with a red mid-drift top. Joe wore a white Gucci t-shirt with his.

Thanks to me, both of our faces were beat to the gawds but I had to admit, he pulled the look off better than me. Joe placed his hair in a ponytail that hung down his back and I rocked a cheek length brown bob. As I glanced at him and remembered my reflection in the mirror, I didn't know why we never considered this before. In my opinion we didn't look like girls, we were prettier than most girls.

"When we get in here you gotta remember what Aunt Stacy said," Joe whispered as we approached the door. He stopped walking and I did too. "Don't go in this school and do the most, Luke. I know how you are and I don't have time for it. Let's stay under the radar, finish high school and go about our business."

I stepped back and tilted my head to the right. I wanted to give this bitch a chance to hear what he was saying. "Girl, I don't know why I gotta keep reminding you that I am not your son."

"It ain't about being my son it's —"

I raised my hand silencing him instantly. "Please carry on with your show, and let me proceed with mine."

"I wouldn't give a fuck, Luke if we weren't in this together. You get caught and I do too."

"You the one who keep forgetting the script, sugar! This is the second time you called me by my government name within five minutes."

"You knew what I meant," he said gripping his notebook to his chest. "We should have as little attention on us as possible, that's all I'm saying."

My lids blinked rapidly before I gave him the wide eye stare. "Speak for yourself." I pointed at him. "The last thing stars can help is the attention they get. Trying to boss me around is gonna be the heaviest load you can bear, so just focus on you."

I gave him the back of my head as I pulled open the doors to the school. The moment we stepped inside it appeared as if all eyes were on us. Girls. Niggas. Everyone appeared to stop and stare at once.

"Oh, my god," Joe whispered. "They know who we are. I knew I should have never agreed to this shit."

I laughed at him. Poor thing wasn't use to having anybody looking his way for more than one minute so he didn't know how to deal with it. "Just follow me," I said confidently.

Realizing they were all probably interested in the new girls at school, I was careful to switch my sexy ass as hard as possible. Joe followed like my little puppy...unsure of life.

When I spotted the 'Office' sign I pointed at it and we both moved toward the entrance. We didn't even know our schedules so it had to be our first stop. Once inside a few girls looked at me and smiled while Joe kept his eyes on the floor. If you ask me he's doing too much to take the spotlight off of himself. It's one thing to stay out of the shine but ignoring the cunts is retarded.

We walked up to the counter, signed our names and sat across from the counter in red plastic chairs. As the seconds dipped by Joe grabbed a magazine off the rack and I fished around in my purse, not really believing that I was holding one out in public, with Joe. Being a girl was so cool. When I located my red lip-gloss I slid it on my lips and dropped it back inside.

Joe looked at me and rolled his eyes. "You don't have to look like a painted up whore to be a girl, Lolita," he whispered. "Damn you gonna ruin this for us. I can just feel it."

I decided to save my voice for all the new people I was going to meet instead of giving him a response. Even as we walked down the hallway I was plotting on the best man to handle me, and I saw a lot of prospects.

I wasn't concerned about getting caught with our paperwork or our new identities. Aunt Stacy was able to get us an emergency hearing to legally change our names to Joanne and Lolita, and afterwards we had our birth certificates and social security cards reflect the new names. She made sure we were set and because of it I felt comfortable.

Within a few minutes a large woman with an angry glare stepped behind the counter, looked at the sign in sheet and said, "Joanne."

When I glanced at my cousin he was too deep in the magazine to hear she was calling him by his fairy name. He so busy telling me to remember what our aunt said and he wasn't even clued in to his 'save face' name. Nudging him a little I said, "She calling you, girl."

He frowned, looked at her and put the magazine back on the rack before hustling toward the counter. "I'm sorry, I didn't hear you." His voice was so low I could barely make out what he was saying.

There was no need to do all of that, lower his voice, because like me, he had a natural feminine tone. All he had to do was talk regular. I shook my head and crossed my legs, realizing that he was the one who was going to fuck this up for us.

"Are you Lolita?" the woman asked pointing at me.

"Yes, that's my cousin." Joe said as if I couldn't respond for myself.

She looked at me and said, "You can come up here too."

I stood up and approached. "Mam?"

"Might as well talk to you both at the same time. I'm Mrs. Holbrook and I'm going to be your guidance counselor." She handed us two small pieces of paper. "These are your schedules and on the back are stickers with your locker numbers and codes. Peel the sticker off and throw it in trash when you've memorized it. You don't want someone breaking into your locker because they will." She eyed both of us, cleared her throat and continued. "Since I'm swamped I'm going to have the School Ambassador show you around."

She turned around and waved a brown skin pretty girl over to us. She had a bone straight weave that hung down her back and pretty long natural eyelashes. She was definitely fly and I liked her immediately.

"Canyetta, please show these young ladies around the school," Mrs. Holbrook said. "They're the new girls."

I caught Canyetta glance at me, taking in my outfit and hair. Within a few seconds I saw her give me a nod of approval. "Cute outfit. Hair too," she said to me. When she looked at Joe he looked away and she rolled her eyes. I guess that would pretty much be the sum of their relationship.

After showing us around we went to our classes with no problem. Most of the other kids seemed laid back and I was surprised everything went so smoothly. I felt like I would fit in here and it didn't take me long to meet a few of Canyetta's friends who were part of the in crowd.

Later that day, when it was time for lunch, Joe and me were standing in line waiting to get our meals when Canyetta found me. "You are going to sit with us," she smiled at me hard. "Because I fucks with you, tough." She looked over at Joe and didn't seem so enthusiastic. "You can hang too if you want but you gotta lighten up a little."

Joe created the fakest smile he could muster and said, "No thank you, I kind of wanted to chill on the first day with my cousin. Maybe next time though."

Why would he lump me in with him? If he wanted to be a bore he would do it alone. "I'm going with her, Joanne," I snapped. "You should come too instead of being so anti." I probably went in too hard around Canyetta but he needed to hear the truth. Plus I didn't want my new friend thinking he could boss me around.

Joe looked at me and shook his head. "You know what, you do what you gotta do." He walked away from the lunch line without getting his food.

"I don't think your cousin likes me," she said as we watched him stomp away.

"Don't worry about her," I said waving Joe off before fingering my bob to make sure it was still in tact. "She'll come around if she wants, and if she doesn't that's okay too."

"I like your personality, you don't care about doing your own thing."

"Pretty much."

After getting my food I watched Joe sitting at a table eating something he bought from the vending machine. I also spotted this really cute nigga smiling his way. When I looked toward Canyetta, preparing to ask her who he was, I saw the heat she was throwing the guy's way.

"Who's that cutie?" I asked.

She was staring so hard at him that she didn't even look at me. "His name's Rico and he's my ex-boyfriend," she said through clenched teeth. Finally she blinked and turned her head toward me. "And if I were you I'd tell your cousin to stay away from him. Even though we not together he's off limits. And I would fuck somebody up over him too."

CHAPTER FIVE

A FEW DAYS LATER

JOE

"It's only been two days and already you disregarding everything Aunt Stacy told us," I said as we walked down the street on the way home from school. I smoothed the side of my hair to make sure my ponytail was still flowing, knowing that in a few days I was going to have to change my style to something else anyway. "You jumped right into her little clique without even knowing what kind of person she is. Are you that hard up to be popular?"

Luke folded his arms over his chest and let out a puff of breath. It was like I was annoying the hell out of him but I didn't care. "Just because you being old in the face don't mean I have to." He paused. "You not even willing to give the girl a chance." He rolled his eyes. "And I love Aunt Stacy but she ain't the one who gotta go to school there. We do. And if we keep ignoring their invitations to go places we gonna be outcasts. And since when has being outcasts ever been a good thing for our social life?"

I stopped walking. "I'm not about to go to no party and you not either, Luke. I can see you now getting drunk and stupid, doing everything in your power to get us caught up. You act like it's gotta be this way forever. All we doing is making sure we can get through the school year, turn eighteen and get our money. Ain't that what you want?"

When Canyetta pulled up in her silver Yukon truck and Luke started squealing and moving excitedly in place like she was a rock star, I got my answer. Since he claimed I was always rude to her I waved but she responded by rolling her eyes. She felt so comfortable being rude I knew they both talked behind my back.

When she parked she focused on him and said, "You rolling with me, Lolita?"

"Where we going?" he asked excitedly.

"Just kicking it with some friends down the bowling alley. Maybe grab a few drinks, one of my chicas is in college and just turned twenty one so we good."

"She's not going to no alley with you, Canyetta," I said seriously. "And she definitely not drinking. So find somebody else to—"

Luke cut his eyes at me like he didn't know me. "Sweetheart, I can go where I want when I want. Remember? You were the one who told me my mother isn't here no more, so be gone."

I grabbed his arm. Looking intensely into his eyes I said, "This girl not good for you. She's trouble, Lolita. I know it."

"You do things your dry ass way and I'll do them mine." He hopped in the truck and they pulled off.

Angry, I stomped my foot and yelled, "Fuck!"

I know the chick mad at me because her little boyfriend, who I told Luke I was not interested in anyway, checks for me every day at lunch. Her problem with me is off center because she needs to run up on Rico. I'm not the one sniffing behind him. It's the other way around.

This whole girl thing is becoming too stressful. I can feel that it's just a matter of time before Luke blows this for the both of us. Now that I think about it every time we get in trouble it's because of him. He was the one who wanted to skip school one day and hook up with two older men who were trying to keep us hostage, in Mississippi when we kept asking to go home. One of them made Luke suck his dick for three hours straight, his lips swollen like large red balloons. The other one made me jerk him off for just as long, my right bicep hurting so much I couldn't move it for days. In the end we ended up escaping out of the bathroom window and getting help. All because when we were walking down the street, they pulled up on us and Luke wanted to 'have fun'.

He was also the one who stole a purse from Macy's because he thought it was cute, even though as far as I knew he wasn't dressing like a girl back then. But the bag wasn't enough, he also had t-shirts and stuffed panties inside of it too. When we were caught I told the security officers I didn't know nothing about it but they weren't hearing it. I was with him so I was in trouble too. If it wasn't for my mother telling the judge that I'd never been in trouble, and was an honor roll student, those charges would still be on my record until I was eighteen.

Sometimes I wish the worse thing possible would happen to Luke so he would be out of my life. I use to hope for his death so bad that I would have to pray just to take it back. I love my cousin but he's too draining.

I was halfway home when an older model black BMW pulled up along side of me. It was Rico and he was so sexy.

I had been doing everything in my power to avoid him, especially after Luke told me he belonged to Canyetta but nothing I did worked. His persistence was relentless and a part of me wanted to give him the time of day because of it. But my plan was to stay low-key and in order to do that I needed to stay away from cute quarterbacks and that meant him.

"So you gonna act like you don't see me?" he asked, as he followed my walking pace in his car. With one hand on the steering wheel and the other stroking his smooth beard, I felt myself getting excited. "Don't act like you don't see me, sexy. But if you want I can play this game as long as you."

"I see you...just don't know what you want from me that's all." I continued to walk hoping he would leave me alone. I'm strong but somebody as cute as him could only bring me to my knees. "Don't you have somebody else to bother? Or some footballs to throw?"

He laughed. "Nothing I'm doing, or nobody I gotta see will be as fine as you."

"Please go away," I said, to weakly to be taken serious.

Instead of pulling off he parked, hopped out and approached me. "Can I at least hold your books?"

"I'm a big girl," I said, avoiding eye contact. I clutched my books harder to my sock stuffed breasts. "I'll be fine." He was so close to me now I could smell some kind of sweet lotion on his skin. Maybe cocoa butter? Or shea butter?

I could feel his prying eyes all over my body. Did he know I was a boy? Was he going to ask me why I was pretending to be someone I wasn't? Suddenly my heart rate increased as he continued to move with me. I wanted to run so that he wouldn't beat me up like so many people wanted to do.

"You're the prettiest thing I've seen in a long time." Relieved it was nothing else, I exhaled loudly. "You okay?" he asked with concern, a warm hand on my back. "Because you look like you want to pass out."

"I'm just trying to do me, Rico." I stopped and looked up at him. His 6'2 inch body appeared to hover over my 5'7 frame. When I realized he was even cuter in person I looked down, away from his gorgeous eyes. As if doing this meant he couldn't see me too. "I don't want to start nothing with nobody. I am a loaner and prefer it that way."

He breathed heavily and when I gazed at him for a moment I saw his nostrils flaring. "That bitch said we were together didn't she? She lied to you and now you believe her. That's why you been giving me a hard time."

I remained quiet.

"Listen, you can't let somebody stop you from getting a nigga who's made for you." He started walking as if he knew my address and like a puppet on a string I moved along. "All I want to do is get to know you. The last thing I would ever do is hurt you or lie about being with a bitch I'm not feeling. That's for suckers and its not how I get down."

"If you not dealing with her she doesn't know it."

He shrugged. "Canyetta is use to getting what she wants. She's not use to somebody telling her no and I guess she sees the way I look at you." He laughed but I didn't catch the joke. "That chick watches everything I do. We only went on two dates and that alone was enough for her to think I was about her."

"So ya'll never fucked?" Where did that come from? I'm supposed to be getting away from him but I find myself falling deeper into his masculinity. Deeper into his conversation. If Luke saw me talking to him I would not hear the end of it. Now I'm so glad he went with Canyetta.

"I never touched that girl," he said firmly. "Like I said, I was gonna give her some love once but she don't know what to say out her mouth. And I'm not into chicks who hang with a lot of people. They bring too much drama and believe it or not, that's not my thing."

I turned the corner leading to my block. As we continued to stroll I couldn't believe he left a perfectly good BMW on the curb to kick rocks with me. I was starting to realize that he wasn't some dumb jock. He was sincerely interested. It was either that or he was doing all he could to get the pussy I didn't have.

I stopped in front of my house and looked over at it. The porch was empty. "So what do you want from me, Rico? Really? I'm not some secretive wild girl who plays quiet during the day, and wilds out at night. What you see right now is what you get. Boring little me."

"I just want you to come to the party my man is having this weekend. Get to know me and form your own conclusions." He paused. "You do that, and if you never want to see me again I'll leave you alone." He squeezed my cheek, the tips of his fingers warm. "Okay, cutie?"

I parted my lips to say yes but he walked away.

When I turned around I saw Aunt Stacy hanging in the doorway with a beer in her palm. How did she get there so quickly? Her dirty pink robe was hanging slightly open revealing a little too much of her left breast. Maybe that's why he got away from me so fast.

Feeling extreme guilt for giving him too much time, I moved toward the door. "He's handsome," she said taking a gulp. "The kind of kid that could make trouble for a girl like you."

"I know," I agreed.

By Paige Lohan

"You have to stay away from him, Joanne. No matter how much you want to believe it, if he finds out you're a boy he will never be with you. He will only hurt you. That's not what you want."

CHAPTER SIX

LUKE

I'm gonna slay them bitches tonight when I slide through the doors of that party!

As I look down at my curves in the blue jeans, white t-shirt and high heels in the mirror I know there won't be a cutie on deck who's not feeling me. And although I wanted my cousin to go too, he made it clear where he stood. He chose to be a hermit and to be honest I think that life is better for him. Not every girl is primed for the limelight.

Besides, last night I spent five hours begging him to go, and telling him why us going would be good for our transgender lives but he wasn't hearing it. Kept saying that he needed to stay away from all things Daniel Day High, and that included Rico's fine ass.

I ran a comb through my bob and glanced at my face, which I put just the right amount of beat on by the way, I was on my way out when Joe walked in and leaned on the doorway. If I wanted to walk out he would be blocking my path.

By Paige Lohan

He stared down at his fingers, which were dressed in red nail polish. "You know this is wrong right? You know that if you go to the party something bad is going to happen?"

I sighed and could feel my jaw clench. "You do realize that you say the same dry shit day after day? You do realize that for much as you talk to me, I still do what I want? Let's face it you're wasting your breath."

"Don't be smart, Luke."

"I'm serious! You spend so much time trying to get me to be you but it never works. Fortunately for you I have an answer." I walked up to him and placed my hand on his forehead. "I hereby excuse Joanne, also known as Joe, from anything that may happen to me." I removed my hand. "Now you can rest easy not having to worry about me and stay your geriatric ass home."

"I thought Aunt Stacy told us not to go."

I grabbed some red Mac Lip Gloss and smoothed it on my puckers. "She changed her mind, plus I did the same thing to her that I did to you. Told her to let me live." I looked him up and down. He was wearing a purple robe and some white fluffy house slippers. We hadn't been here for a week and already he was dressing like an old maid. "You are starting to look like her you know?"

"Who?" he asked, eyebrows raised.

"Aunt Stacy," I placed the gloss down and grabbed my purse. "It's sad because with your looks you could bring all the boys to the yard. If I were you I would come with me, but whether you do or not won't make a difference as far as I'm concerned. Because this bad bitch is going and she's going to serve too."

He sighed. "You aren't afraid of saying the wrong thing? Or getting so drunk that you'll make a mistake and somebody will find out who you really are?"

I was now realizing what Joe's issue was and I felt sad for him. He wasn't trying to be dry; he just didn't know how to live on the edge. He was afraid to have fun because he was always worried about something happening.

After my mother died and I first moved to his house, I spent six months in the room not going anywhere. All because he kept saying how he heard some crazy white man was running around town killing gay black boys. It wasn't until I started talking to my classmates that I found out there was only one incident of a white man murdering a gay black boy in my town, and he was dead.

"You are right, if I go out there is a possibility that something bad will happen. But I'm more afraid of not living my life." I walked over to him and grabbed his hand. "Joe, this is what you want, I can see it in your eyes. Finally we're in a place where we don't have to hide from the spotlight. Come with me and enjoy it."

"But we aren't being ourselves. We're liars."

"The world is full of fucking liars!" I yelled letting his hand go. "Even though we wearing wigs and a little makeup we have always been this way." I raised my hands and ran them down my curves. "We have always been feminine. The only thing I'm mad about is not doing this a long time ago. Had we thought about this I could've been living my life and would probably have a boyfriend by now."

"It's dangerous."

I rolled my eyes and a plan popped into mind. He wanted to go to this party but he needed a reason...somebody he could save. For tonight I'll let it be me. "Listen, all I'm going to do is go to the party, have a few drinks, smoke a little weed and —"

He walked deeper into the room and stood before me. "What you talking about?" he yelled, eyes widening. "You can't do that shit! If I know one thing about you it's that you can't hold your liquor and high at the same time."

I looked at him slyly. "Too bad you won't be there to save me."

Silence filled the room and I could sense the words he wanted to say rising from his throat and sitting on the tips of his lips. He looked at me through lowered brows. "I know what you doing, bitch. You not slick."

I laughed. "Seriously, if you won't go with me, who will save me?"

"I'm getting dressed now." He said as he walked out of the room.

I shook my head and laughed, having accomplished my mission so easily.

Forty minutes later, after I did his makeup, we were both in the living room with our Aunt Stacy and her boyfriend Toppy. He was an overweight guy who didn't say a word to us unless it was through clenched teeth. Even now he gazed at me like he hated me, although I didn't understand why.

"You two look gorgeous!" Stacy said as she placed her hands over her lips. She turned her head toward her man. "Don't they, honey?"

Toppy grabbed a pack of cigarettes off the table, pulled one out and lit it before taking a hard pull. "What I tell you about putting me in this shit?" he took another pull and smoke wafted out into the living room. " What I tell you about my stance on you changing two black boys into sissies?"

"Excuse me?" Joe snapped as he placed his hands on his hips.

"Son, I don't mean no disrespect, but what you two doing is wrong," he continued. "It wouldn't be a problem if people who came in contact with you knew what they were getting, but as it turns out you're both liars. What kind of way is that to live?"

"Toppy, these are my nephews and you don't have the right to make them feel that way!" Aunt Stacy yelled. "Now I know you don't like it but trying to make them feel worse about a decision that I made is cruel."

He stood up. "As long as you have them dressing like girls and lying you will never understand the damage you've done. Something bad is going to happen behind this, Stacy. Young men don't like being lied to, or teased by boys who do a good job of faking it as girls."

"Well thanks for the compliment anyway," I said sarcastically.

"Luke, just leave it alone!" Joe said.

"Why?" I could hear my blood pounding in my years. "This nigga got to say everything he wanted."

Toppy rushed over to me and looked down into my eyes. I don't know how he moved so quickly but Joe was right next to me. It felt like the room was spinning until Joe jumped in front of him, both of us overpowered by Toppy's 6'4 inch height and large body.

"Like I said, if you continue to lie something very terrible is going to happen to both of you." He looked into my eyes and then Joe's. "You have been warned by the only person in this room who really gives a fuck." He walked out of the house and slammed the door.

CHAPTER SEVEN

JOE

Somehow I was given a deck of cards and before I knew it five people surrounded me, wowed at my ability to guess the card they picked every time. All of my life I enjoyed doing magic and as the years went by it was the only thing that made me feel good about myself.

Surprisingly I had been here for two hours and was having a good time, with my cousin nowhere in sight. Even though I was worried about not knowing where he was I was having fun. Guess Luke was right about me coming out. I was just about to do another trick when Rico came inside the party, looking so delicious. Wearing designer jeans, a fresh white t-shirt and black rosary beads, the simplicity of his outfit was refreshing.

"What you got going on here?" he asked with all of the people surrounding me.

"She's some magician," Courtney said as she sipped her drink. "We been stuck here all night wondering how she does this shit."

"Mind if she entertains me for a little while?" He was authoritative and kind and that was also a turn on. I was starting to get the feeling that there wasn't anything he could do wrong. Without another word, the five of them rose and disappeared into the party.

He sat next to me and I could feel the heat steaming from his body. His breath smelling like a pack of double mint gum. His eyes glancing over me made my heart skip. Did I look cute enough? Should I have worn something a little sexier, or toned it down a bit? The questions flipped around in my mind like a fish on dry land and I wanted to appear more confident.

More like my cousin.

"You look sexy," he whispered, moving an inch closer. "Good thing I got here when I did, I can see some nigga trying to scoop you up now."

My mouth opened, jaw hung and my tongue felt like it disappeared into my throat. He was so into me and I didn't feel worthy. With him I could never do the right thing, say the right thing or be the right thing. It was like we were dancing, except my feet weren't moving and he had to carry me. "I'm okay," I looked down at myself, preparing to point out many of my flaws. "I was going to wear something else but I just grabbed this."

"Good choice," he winked.

That's when shit went wrong.

My dick got hard.

Had I even suspected something like this would happen I would've never come but now it was too late. I could feel myself swelling in my pants and my eyes expanded as I tried to find a place to run. I would've preferred one of my socks to fall out of my bra than this.

"Sexy, you listening to me?" he asked, sitting so close now that our knees touched. He placed his warm hand on my leg, too close to my crotch. And it was then that I noticed the fruity smell of alcohol on his breath. Maybe he wouldn't notice my stiffness.

"I'm fine, I just...you know...am shy."

"You sure, because I'm getting the impression that you don't want to be bothered. Why do you make me feel like that?"

"I...I...don't know what you want me to say." I wiped the sweat forming on my forehead and made sure my purse stayed in my lap. I needed to do something to stop being aroused. I pushed my thoughts toward my mother, and her cancer. Surely wasn't anything sexy about that. "You know I like you, that's why I'm here. I just, I guess I move slower than other girls that's all."

"What you doing after you leave here, Joanne?"

My right foot moved rapidly as if the floor was hot. I probably looked ridiculous. Inexperienced and nerd-like but when I glanced his way he didn't seem to notice. "Right now I don't have any plans." I shrugged. "I don't usually stay out late so I may just go home."

He laughed. "Don't count the night out just yet, I'm trying to change that." He smiled brighter and tilted his head slightly. Was he trying to kiss me? "And you should know that I almost always get what I want."

"You sound like Canyetta now. Maybe you two are perfect for each other after all."

"Listen at you," he grinned. "I told you my mind is made up already about who I'm feeling. Oh, and you should also know that I don't give up easily. Which basically means that as long as I have my eyes on you, which I do, there ain't nothing I won't do to make you mine."

I smiled but wiped it away. The more he talked the more aroused I got. Never in my wildest dreams did I think I would win the attention of the most popular dude in high school, but here it was happening. I felt like I was in the movies and since I didn't see it before I wasn't sure how it would end.

"What do you want me to say? I mean, I gotta ask my aunt and if she says yes I don't see a problem with hanging out." I took a deep breath and looked at him. I wanted to exert some power over the situation but his stare was intense and once again I turned my head toward the crowd, away from him. "Why are you so interested? I like your attention, don't get me wrong, but I don't get it."

He chuckled softly. "I'm going to be honest, first off you're beautiful. And I liked that you're quiet."

"Why? You afraid I'll find out who you really are?"

"Not about that. It's more about not liking loose chicks. Broads who do anything for a nigga to slide them some dick. The quieter the better for me."

"You making a lot of assumptions before—"

I couldn't finish my sentence because when I glanced across the living room, by the stairs, I saw

Luke walking up them with Thomas, who happened to be Rico's cousin. Thomas was tall and lanky who along with this kid name Carlo, sold weed at our school. Although he wasn't as scary as Carlo, who had a patch of blond hair going down the middle of his bald scalp, he was still bad news. Thomas pushed a Benz and had a little cash, which was probably the only reason Luke was going upstairs with him.

As I watched closer I could see Luke was leaning all over him, and it looked like he had way too much to drink and smoke. Just when I started to let my hair down this bitch does something to ruin everything. I started to let her go upstairs and do whatever, but I didn't want the slack coming back my way.

I hopped up and rushed over to them, grabbing Luke roughly by the arm. "What you doing? Ain't nothing upstairs that could be better than what's going on down here."

Thomas slapped my hand away. "Hold up, shawty. She going with me."

I pushed him back so hard that he knocked up against the wall. As easy as it was to shove him I could tell he was drunk too. "This my cousin! Fuck you

By Paige Lohan

talking about hold up? She had way too much to drink and don't need to be going upstairs with you."

"Don't do this shit, girl!" Luke snapped at me. "It's my business and you need to tend to yours." She looked over my shoulder at Rico who I didn't know was there.

"Hey, cuz, why don't you chill down here," Rico suggested to Thomas. "If Joanne got a problem with ya'll being alone maybe you don't need to go."

Thomas looked at Luke and said, "You rolling or not, Lolita?"

Luke looked at me and with a sly smile on her face said, "We should've kept it moving anyway instead of wasting time on them." She looked at him. "Let's go, boo the more time we spend here the less fun we going to have."

Thomas walked up the steps with Luke and I could feel my skin growing hot. When I turned around Rico was staring at me. "Everything gonna be cool." he said stroking my shoulders. "He won't do anything to her she doesn't want to happen."

"That's the problem." The only good thing about all of this was that now my dick was soft.

LUKE

I was lying face down on somebody's bed as Thomas eased in and out of my asshole. His strokes felt like repeated massage strokes and my body shivered every time he moaned. I convinced him to fuck me this way, saying I got my period even though he said constantly that he didn't care.

"Hit that shit just like that," I said wiggling my ass around so he could go deeper.

I had my hands stuffed under my body, my dick cupped in my palm. I was protecting it closely, and if Joe was here he'd probably be proud of me because I was keeping the secret safe. As he moved in and out of me I was pushing into my palm and I could feel myself about to cum.

"Damn, this shit tight," he said, hot breath steaming up the back of my neck. I could feel his body pulsate, and even though he was probably a hoe, it felt good to have someone want you with that much passion. "I wish I could fuck you face to face though. Let me do you right, I don't care if you on your period.

By Paige Lohan

You don't look like one of them dirty chicks, let me hit it anyway." He was begging and it was sexy.

"I told you I don't fuck on my cycle. The only reason I'm doing this is because I wanted you so bad I made an exception." The more talking I was doing the harder it was for me to get to that special place. "Just keep moving, daddy. Because the shit feels good on my end."

As he continued to stroke I tightened my asshole even more and could hear him moan each time I did. "Oh my fucking gawd! What you doing?" he paused. "I'm gonna marry your pretty ass. Bet, you gonna be my wife and have my babies."

Hearing him talk that sweet shit in my ear caused my asshole to juice up. Laying claim to me behind my fuck game meant I had the power to keep a nigga's heart. If being a girl felt this good I couldn't wait to see what else life had in store for me.

He was throbbing. And when I felt him about to cum I decided to help him a little by backing up harder. I got so into it that I gripped the pillows on the side of my head and rubbed my shit off on the bed. The motion caused me to be able to bust and I bit down on my bottom lip. "I'm cumming, Thomas, please don't stop. I...I'm almost there." Suddenly I felt myself explode into somebody's bed as I could feel him going harder for his.

"I'm almost there too, pretty bitch," he said moaning heavily. "Just keep bucking that ass the way you do and I'll be there in no time."

I was still coming down off my nut when he snaked his hands around my waist, his fingertips brushing the tip of my limp wet dick. I think he was going for my pussy.

Oh shit! Now there was trouble.

"What the fuck?" he yelled getting up. His eyes were huge and I thought if he spread them anymore the balls would pop out and fall to the floor. Looking down at me he pointed and said, "What was that...what was...what did I just touch?"

I balled up on my side and snatched a pillow that smelled like sour milk to cover my penis. Now that I think about it everything in the room stunk, maybe I was coming down off my liquor and weed high, finally seeing things for what they really were...a mess.

"It's nothing, Thomas." I sat up on the edge of the bed and looked back at him. "Why you tripping when we were having so much fun? Come back over here and get yours off because I know you didn't cum yet."

I could tell in his eyes that the last thing he was interested in was fucking me. I don't know why but I had visions of this happening before. In my dream I would imagine me dressing up in drag, having sex with some hottie as a girl and them finding out I was a boy. But each time they found out nobody ever left, besides, it felt too good to them. In my mind better than the real thing, so why was he tripping?

He walked up to me, snatched the pillow and said, "You a fucking dude? Tell me!" His nostrils flared and I watch his fingers crawl into tight fists. His chin rose high and I could tell that things would not end good. "Answer my fucking question."

My fingers still protected my penis. "Why you looking so crazy? We were having fun and —"

"Bitch, stop fucking around with me for I kill your ass in here! Are you a dude or not?"

Tiring of playing games I stood up, my hands still covering my balls. For some reason my toes curled up as I tried to think things through. When I realized there was no way out I dropped my hands to my sides, revealing my limp dick. "Are you happy now?" I asked, arms rising in the air. "I was trying to protect your feelings but fuck it."

He walked over to the corner of the room and threw up. With one hand on the wall and the other on his gut I watched him heave for two minutes before turning around to look at me. He wiped the back of his mouth. "I can't believe this shit."

I waved the air. "Cut the bullshit, sugar. You knew I was a guy so don't even act shocked."

He walked away from the corner, slowly, almost like a crawl. When he stood in front of me I realized his expression was blank and that scared me more. I didn't see his fist coming until it was too late, landing strongly in the middle of my right eye. I dropped to the bed and tried to take in the pain. It was blinding, piercing and stabbing, which caused my entire body to sweat.

He shook his hand and placed his jeans on. "I'm gonna tell everybody you a nigga! Everybody!" He held the sides of his face and paced the floor. It was like he was talking to himself and I just happened to be in the room. "I can't believe this shit! I can't believe I just fucked a dude! I'm not even gay! Why would you

By Paige Lohan

play with somebody like that? Huh? Are you that fucking crazy?"

I laughed, as I could feel my eye swelling up. "If you fucked a dude, honey it means you are gay."

He rushed up to me. "You gonna die for this shit!"

I rolled over and looked up at him with my good eye. "Relax because I'm gonna tell you what's going to happen." I stood up; doing my best to pretend that his blow didn't hurt me, even though my vision was partially taken. "You are going to go to school tomorrow and act normal. Then you gonna keep what happened between us quiet, never telling a soul." I placed my hands on my hips. "If you don't do exactly as I say, I'm telling everybody, and I mean *everybody*, that you ain't nothing but a shit chaser. I wonder how many friends you would have then?" I laughed, placed my clothes on and walked around him. He was stiff like a statue, probably taking in every word I said. "Oh, and before I forget. You got that one hit off on me, but best believe you will never get another." I walked out.

CHAPTER EIGHT

JOE

I left the party a little while after Luke walked upstairs with Thomas. Now sitting in his bedroom I was trying to understand why he could be so reckless. I would've sat outside the door but Rico's concern for my feelings irritated me. He wouldn't let me breathe. Not wanting to take it out on him I figured it would be best to bounce when he wasn't looking, so I did.

Now here I am, pacing the floor in my cousin's room waiting for the moment to talk to Luke. All I want to know is if he had sex and more than anything if the secret was still safe.

Instead of calm, the moment I saw him I stole him in the mouth with a fist I didn't even know I formed. It took me a minute to see that his eye was already bruised, turning black. I wonder how that happened. It wouldn't have mattered anyway because I could no longer sit back and act like shit was okay.

My mind went quickly on the past.

I thought about how he always came between my mother and me. How since he lived with me I had

By Paige Lohan

to share her love even though it was rightfully mine. I thought about how he made friends so easily at my school, while I had been there for years and had gone unnoticed. Before I knew it rage bubbled at the surface of my skin and I fought him as if we didn't share the same blood. As if he was a nigga off the street. And the way he was acting I felt warranted.

Rolling around on the floor we scratched and clawed at each other's faces. I was doing my best to mess up his beauty, hoping that people would see him for who he really was, a scared little boy who didn't care who he hurt. Five minutes later I noticed I didn't have the same energy anymore. I was done with Luke and the trouble that always seemed to follow him.

Barely able to breathe, I crawled on top of his bed, my body collapsing to the side. He moved to the corner of the room and leaned up against the wall. "Everything you touch…everything you come near you ruin," I said.

He took a deep breath, his head dropping momentarily before lifting it back up. "You were ruined before I came into your life, Joe. And now you know it."

I hated him so much I could spit in his face. Instead I sat up, my elbows planted on my thighs. "You don't give a fuck about nobody but yourself. On second thought, you don't even like yourself." My breaths were still rapid but slower. "We haven't been here a month and already you doing all the things that got us in trouble back home. What's wrong with you? Why does everything have to be drama?" I looked into his eyes, one swollen and the other darkening by the minute, hoping he could make me understand.

Instead he laughed hysterically and wiped the blood off of his lips. I knew then that he was beyond crazy. "You know what your problem is girl, you can't stand for nobody to have fun. You expect everybody to move cautiously. To be scared. Just because I ain't boring doesn't mean something is wrong with me, Joe. Tell the truth, if you had it your way you would trade places with me wouldn't you? In a heartbeat, honey! Because I'm the one person in your world who reminds you that you will never amount to anything."

My neck stiffened and I could feel myself wanting to tell him of the secrets he didn't know I knew. I wanted to tell him what my mother told me about why she had to let him stay all the nights I begged her to put him out. The truth sat on my tongue and if I hadn't promised my mother, with what was left of her dying soul, I would tell him right now and bust his world.

"The last person on earth I want to be like is you, Luke. You think the only way you can get attention is if you fuck and suck boys off. But it never works does it? You even tried it with Marcus and what happened, huh? What he do to us?" I paused. "I don't even have to tell you, because you know the rest."

"You don't know what you talking about!" he yelled, and I knew I struck a nerve.

"I saw you and him in his car, so keep it real Luke. The day we raided ma's liquor cabinet and the three of us sat in the diner and got drunk off vodka. We were all about to walk out but I had to double back into the diner. Ya'll walked out without me and went to the car."

I saw his eyes lighten up. I guess he was realizing I knew more than he thought. Or maybe he was surprised that I hid what I knew for so long, since he could never keep a secret.

"What you don't know is that all the bathrooms were full, so I walked outback, where Marcus' car was parked and pissed on the side of the dumpster. At first

I thought Marcus was by himself, until I saw his neck drop backwards, your head in his palm." Now I was the one laughing like a fool even though I saw nothing funny. He looked away from me and I knew I had him. Now he was the weaker one.

"You wrong," he said quietly. "You don't know everything, Joe. That's always been your problem."

He wouldn't admit it, even now while I had him backed in the corner with the truth. "My eyes don't lie!"

"It didn't happen that way," he said a bit louder. "You saw what you saw but things aren't always what they seem."

"So I guess you weren't fucking your own father either? I guess that wasn't the real reason my aunt killed him, because she caught you two together? I know all about that situation, Luke, so don't come for me." The moment I breathed the words my mother shared with me I wished I could take them back. I had betrayed her trust just to get at my cousin and now I wasn't sure if it was worth it.

Huge tears rolled down his cheeks as if he had held them, knowing this would come. "Yes it's true, I was giving Marcus head in the car, but what you don't know is that he raped me. Made me do it."

"Stop lying!"

"It's true! He had been coming onto me about five days before that happened and I wouldn't give in. I kept telling him no and to leave me alone."

"Yeah right, since when do you ever not give in? Everybody knows you a whore."

"And even a whore has feelings, Joe." His voice was softer, almost like a whisper. "Even a whore wants friends and I didn't want to ruin what the three of us had together." He stared at the ceiling. "I remember that day too, at the diner. And I remember I didn't want to go in the first place. You had to beg me, promising to buy my food if I went."

"You always like to have fun so why was that time different?"

"Well I didn't want to go this time because Marcus and me had a fight the day before, in the gym. He wanted me to have sex with him, saying that he knew a few dudes who I let hit. I told him I liked him as a friend, and wanted us to stay cool but he didn't care. He grew so mean, Joe," he continued finally looking at me. "He looked like the same monster he was the day in the cafeteria."

My mouth was open, as I didn't know what to believe. "If that was true you couldn't ask for help? You could've told somebody."

"I tried to tell you," he said softly. "I begged you to let me stay home and you didn't. Peer pressured me and everything. So what you didn't see was as I was sucking him off he held a knife to the back of my neck. I was raped, Joe, I swear to God."

The room felt like it was spinning around.

Luke wiped his tears away roughly and looked over at me. "And my father raped me every day I can remember. I begged my mother to call the police but she was afraid because she was a drug dealer, with a felony on her record. She thought no one would believe her, and figured she'd handle it herself. What you don't know is that Aunt Poochy knew what was going down before it did. My mother made sure with yours that I would be taken care of and then she killed my father and then herself."

"What if I don't believe you?" I said, despite holding on to his every word.

"I don't give a fuck what you believe, Joe!" he wiped tears away roughly with his fist. "If you don't like how I'm living don't say shit else to me. It's really that simple."

"Is that how you want it?"

"I am over this whole production!" he yelled. "Like you said, I don't care about nobody but myself and I'm tired of apologizing for it."

I stood up. "If something happens to you I'm gonna laugh over your grave, bitch." I pointed at him.

He stood up, got in my face and spit blood all over my nose. I went ballistic. This time the plan was to break the lamp on his dresser, grab a broken piece and hit his jugular. As I reached for it I was suddenly whisked up in the air by Toppy.

When did he get in here?

With what felt like super human strength, he tossed me across the room and pushed Luke back with a firm shove to the chest. "What the fuck is going on in here, little niggas?" When I looked behind him I saw my Aunt Stacy standing in the doorway.

"Nothing," I said walking around him. "I'm leaving anyway." I stomped out of Luke's room.

When I made it to my bedroom it took fifteen minutes for me to calm down, and when I finally did I realized I couldn't live here anymore. Things were too painful. Too much going on. A part of me felt guilty about what he said about being raped, especially if it's true. But Luke acts so fucked up that I don't know what to believe, or what to feel.

For once in my life it was about my sanity, and if I wanted to keep it I had to steer clear of Luke.

I was just about to take a shower when my phone rang. I picked it up and said, "What?"

"Wow, you don't seem happy to hear from me," Rico said, his tone more upbeat than I felt. "I knew I didn't chill with you long enough to put you in a good mood."

Suddenly I felt a need to smile. "I'm sorry. It's been a long night."

"I know, you left without saying goodbye. I went to get you a drink and they said you snuck out the back door." He laughed a little. "I hope you didn't let my cousin get you angry. He can be a bitch type nigga at times but you should never let him get to you."

I sighed and sat on the edge of the bed. "My cousin ain't no better. He don't know what to do with himself

By Paige Lohan

half of the time." I realized my elbows throbbed and tried to think of what move I created to cause so much pain.

"He?" Rico said. "Did you just say he?"

I swallowed the lump in my throat and suddenly things seemed blurry. After all this time I said Luke would be the one to give away our secret and here it was, me letting it all out over the phone. "I...uh...I was talking about Thomas. Just changed up a little in the convo and confused you that's all."

He was silent for a few seconds. "What you doing now?"

"Nothing."

"Well look outside. I'm out front. Let me get you away, and don't say no."

CHAPTER NINE

JOE

We were sitting on the back steps of Rico's house kicking it. A few mosquitos tried their best to get at my arms and I waved them around every so often, almost slapping him in the face once. No matter what I did, or how I moved, his eyes were always all over me.

Every time I tried to enjoy myself, enjoy him, my thoughts swirled back around to my cousin. Now I felt guilty for some of the things I said.

"You gonna tell me what you thinking about?" he put his arm around me, and I moved into him. "Gonna tell me what has you so sad, because it can't be your cousin still."

What am I doing here?

"You must be use to people telling you everything, even if it's private." I smiled. "What can I say, I don't want to talk about it, Rico. And I know I should not have come here but there was no place else I wanted to be."

He nodded. "Everything's a struggle with you isn't it?"

"If it is I don't know, I guess that makes it worse huh?"

"At the party, when I came up behind you and asked if you were okay, you looked at me like you were about to tell me something. I've been around people who hold things back but have never seen it so strong before. What is it, Joanne. And what do you want to say but keep stopping yourself?" He touched my hand and I trembled.

"Remember when you first tried to kick it with me? And we were walking down the street, leading to my house?"

"I do."

"I told you then that I was boring. I told you then that I wasn't some secretive wild child behind closed doors." My spine bent forward as my elbows pressed into my thighs. "It's like you want me to be somebody I'm not. What you see right now is all there is. Can you accept that? Because if you can't I promise my feelings won't be hurt." I exhaled because it was a lie. "I'm kind of expecting you to walk away."

"Now look who's expecting someone to be what they aren't." he laughed. "It's not in my nature to walk away from anything," he winked. "I'm an athlete, don't forget that."

Trying to skip the subject I said, "Tell me something you never told another person, not even Canyetta."

"I have a dictionary full of things I never told her." He took his arm from around me and scooted his body so that he could get a good look. There he goes with the staring again.

"Well just give me one thing."

"Something embarrassing?"

"Both."

We both laughed.

"Okay, well, when I was in the 9th grade I kissed my school teacher."

"So she raped you?" I asked, as I positioned my body so that I could look at him.

"No, no it wasn't nothing like that," he waved his hand.

"Sounds pretty creepy to me."

He laughed. "I actually fell coming up the steps, taking some flowers to this girl named Crew.

By Paige Lohan

That was the first embarrassing part of my day. We had some dumb party that week and she promised to go with me. My father suggested I bring her some roses, since it was Valentines Day and she said no twenty times before finally agreeing. Now that I think about it I should never have listened to him. He's a veteran who collects guns for a living. But here I was letting him give me girl advice."

I found myself laughing and realized I was having more fun than I had in a long time.

"Anyway I got up and walked them up to her, in the hallway, and she went off on me in front of everybody," he continued. "Saying the only reason she told me she was going with me was so that I would leave her alone. I have never been more embarrassed." He was laughing so hard he was crying. "So I drop them mothafuckas on the ground and rushed to Homeroom just to get away from everybody. My teacher was in there alone and asked what was wrong. I guess she felt sorry for me, gave me a hug and I landed one on her lips." He was now laughing so hard he was reddening and his sound made me laugh. "I was in detention for one week behind that shit."

I wiped my eyes, wet with tears from laughter. But I was also impressed that he chose to tell me a story where he didn't get the girl. He was more down to earth than I realized.

"Was that really embarrassing?"

"What you think?" he said nudging me.

"Okay, tell me another one."

"Well this one is going to sound crazy but it's not like that."

"I'll be the judge of that," I joked.

"Well, I passed your house before, on the way home from school a while back. I go that way sometimes. Anyway a few weeks before you and your cousin enrolled in school I saw two boys walk into the house. Who were they? Your boyfriends?"

My stomach bubbled and my jaw hung. I knew this was a bad idea. Aunt Stacy said we needed to be careful and here I was, allowing him to tell me all of the things I wanted to hear. All of the things I thought would take my mind off of the fact that soon, very soon, this bubble I lived in, the one where I claimed to be a girl, would bust.

By Paige Lohan

I should use the moment to tell him the truth, like I was going to at the party. Instead I said, "You sure it was my house?"

"Positive," he said firmly.

When a silver Yukon pulled up his eyes got big as saucers. Just like that I didn't seem to be as important anymore and I was grateful. The funny thing is I've seen that truck before but with everything going on I couldn't figure out from where. "I can't believe she came by here," he said through clenched teeth. "This the last thing I need right now."

"Who is that?" I squinted looking at the truck park.

He looked at me as if telling me would hurt my feelings. "Canyetta."

I touched the base of my neck. "Canyetta? I thought you said ya'll didn't fuck with each other." My eyes narrowed. "Is this all a game? You been playing me the whole time hoping I would fuck you so you could go back to her? I been going at it all night with Lolita, the last thing I need is this."

He stood up and grabbed me by the hand. "Quick, come inside and when she leaves I'll come and get you." He led me through the back door, into the kitchen and I took a seat in a yellow cushion chair. "I'm sorry how it looks but it's not like that between us." His eyebrows gathered in a pained expression. "I wouldn't fuck up with you for her, I promise."

My body felt heavy, like I was being played. "I just want to go home, Rico. That's it."

"But I don't want you to. Give me five minutes and after that you can leave." He kissed me on the lips, cut the lights off and dipped out the door, making sure to close it behind him.

And there I sat, stupidly; waiting for the guy I just met to come back and get me. What if he had so much fun he forgot I was there? My legs moved rapidly and suddenly I needed to see them together. I needed to know that he didn't want her as much as he claimed, even though it should not have made a difference.

So I stood up, walked toward the window and slowly moved the curtains. Not a lot, just enough to see what I needed. Carefully I eased my fingers into a slit on the venetian blinds and pulled it down. My belly felt knotted as I saw her sitting on his lap, touching his face.

This is all dumb! If he wanted her there was no need for me to hide in here to make things easier. Full of jealousy, I opened the door and stepped outside. My

By Paige Lohan

arms crossed over my body, protecting my heart. "I want to go home," I said looking over their heads.

With wide eyes filled with hate she said, "Oh hold up, what the fuck she doing here, Rico? Huh? Why would you bring this chick here when you said you wanted to give me another chance?"

"No, bitch, *you said* you wanted me to give you another chance. He pushed her off of his lap and she stumbled backwards. "Anyway I told you I had company, and that you had to leave. But you sat on my lap and wouldn't bounce. Now you got your feelings hurt and it's my fault?" He shook his head. "Yo, shawty, get the fuck up off my porch before I stun your ass."

Instead of going off on him she ran up to me and yanked my arm. I was quickly pulled down the steps and sucked into a fight that wasn't mine. I may have not been stronger than most dudes but next to a girl it wasn't a match. I took a closed fist and brought it down over her nose, opening it up instantly.

I was about to finish her off when Rico lifted her up and tossed her across the yard, something like I saw Toppy do earlier. "Get the fuck out of my house!" he pointed at her truck.

A School of Dolls   105

"So you gonna let that manly bitch hit me and not do nothing about it?"

"Canyetta, go, now!" Everybody within a mile could probably tell by the tone of his voice that he was serious. She stood up, dusted herself off and tried to come for me again before he pushed her several feet backwards. "I'm not fucking around!"

Breathing heavily she said, "You gonna pay for this." Her eyes were on me. "Death is gonna come to you, whore! Watch!"

"Bitch, kick rocks!" he yelled.

She backed up, stared at me and then at him. "This bitch will never love you as much as I do. And you're going to see that soon." She looked at me and took a deep breath. "You can have him, whore, because I'm done!" She ran to her truck.

When we heard the door slam followed by two gunshots, we both ducked and could hear her pulling off.

I held my hand over my heart, wondering if it was still there. I may be a country bumpkin but we don't have stuff like this going on around my neighborhood.

Slowly he turned around, I guess making sure she was gone before walking over to me. "You okay?" He held my arms.

"Take me home," I said seriously. "Because if this is your idea of having fun I'm not with it."

"Joanne, please don't go," he pleaded. "Don't let a stupid bitch ruin our night when we were having a good time, getting to know each other and shit." He looked into my eyes. "The only thing I want to do is spend some time with you."

I looked down and crossed my arms over my body. "What do you want from me, Rico?" My chest felt tight. "I told you I'm not about the drama and here I am dealing with it anyway. I almost got shot."

"She wasn't gonna shoot shit."

"You don't know that!"

"Yes I do because I would fuck her up." He paused. "Come upstairs with me and talk. Just five minutes. And then if you want to dip I will take you home myself, I promise."

He wasn't use to hearing no, and now I knew why. He talked so good he didn't have to.

CHAPTER TEN

JOE

Don't ask me how it happened because I'm not sure.

One minute I wanted to leave and would have called 911 if he didn't let me go. And the next I was standing on my knees in the corner of Rico's room with his dick in my mouth. Every so often he would try to touch my head, covered in a wig, and I would slap his hands and threaten to stop. After awhile he gave up, maybe afraid unlike the last ten times I said I wanted to go, that this time I would actually leave.

Still, how did I get to this? Being sexual with a guy I actually liked for the first time in my life. The last thing I remembered was trying to fight him off of having sex with me, even though I wanted nothing more. I even thought about a few ways we could do it, although all of them ended up with him touching my penis and getting insanely mad.

Before long I invited him to a blowjob. I may have never given one before but for some reason I was

By Paige Lohan

a natural. I licked, sucked and jerked him to a point where he could hardly stand up.

Hearing him moan caused my dick to throb. And the more he begged me not to stop, the closer I was to reaching an orgasm myself. "You feel so good, Joanne, I wish I could touch you." His body trembled like he was convulsing. "Please, let me get inside you for five minutes. I don't want to cum like this."

"No," I said with him still in my mouth, resting on my tongue.

The more he begged, the hornier I got until I did cum without being touched. I didn't have enough time to be embarrassed, because I was still trying to get him off too. I wanted him satisfied. The best part about me reaching mine meant that I didn't have to worry about a stiff penis through my jeans…just a wet stain, which I would explain some how if he asked.

"I'm almost there, baby, fuck, I'm almost there." Before I knew it semen poured down my throat and I swallowed every ounce, doing my best not to gag from the thick creamy load. When I was done I looked up at him and he helped me to my feet, walking me over to the edge of the bed. "Oh, my gawd…that was the…that was the first time I ever…"

"You lying," I said wiping my mouth with the back of my hand. "You don't need to give me compliments. I'm good."

He moved to a small refrigerator, handed me a coke and sat next to me. "Joanne, I never had anybody do that to me. Didn't you see how I could barely stand up? You turned my legs into noodles."

I popped the Coke open and took a long gulp, to wash his cum down. "Anybody would've done that to you, just for you to..." my voice trailed off and I started feeling stupid again. Why didn't confidence last long enough in my heart so that I would have it all night?

He grabbed a red towel, wiped his dick and placed his clean hand on my thigh. "What were you about to say? Stop biting your tongue."

"I was going to say, that, that anybody would do that to you, just so you would look at them, the way you look at me."

He smiled. "You make me seem like a king, when if you knew me you'd know I'm anything but." He kissed me on the cheek. "Why were you so, so sexy about it? I felt like you could've been down there all night if I asked."

110   By Paige Lohan

He was right. "I just wanted you to feel good," I said blushing. He moved closer, and eased his hand further up my thigh, inches away from my wet stain. "Please don't do this, Rico." I stopped his hand. "I mean what else do you want? I satisfied you right?"

"I want to return the favor." He kissed me on the neck. "Come on, baby, let me eat your pussy or something."

He wouldn't stop and now I was irritated. I jumped up and grabbed my purse. "I have to go."

He stood up and fumbled around for his pants. "Wait, you just got here."

"I've been here for hours remember, we were outside first, before your girlfriend showed up." I moved toward the door, fumbling with the lock to let myself out.

"Joanne, at least let me take you home." With one leg in his jeans he grabbed his keys off the floor and hopped toward me. Now he was the one who looked ridiculous and for some reason I found that cute.

"No, I want to be a fucking lone!" I walked out and slammed the door. I didn't want to be so brutal but I had to be serious so he would not convince me to have sex with him and blow my cover. I wasn't as strong as he was. I got the feeling he could get me to do anything he wanted.

As I stormed out of his house tears poured down my face. Why did God make me like this? Why was everything about me feminine except my penis? It felt like I never got what I wanted, ever.

When I made it outside I was surprise to see Toppy's navy blue pick up truck in the front of Rico's house. At first I thought it was a mistake until he waved me over. Walking up to it I leaned in the open window and asked, "What are you doing here? How did you even know where I was?"

"Get inside," he said with a straight face, before reaching for his pack of cigarettes from the glove compartment.

Reluctantly I tugged the truck's handle but it wouldn't open so I pulled it again. Once inside I hopped up in the seat, closed the door and crossed my arms over my chest. This seemed too weird, like it wasn't really happening. "How did you know I was here?"

"When you left the house, after fighting Luke, I followed you. I left and came back a few times in case you needed a ride. So here I am again. And here you are."

I hope he didn't like me or nothing.

I looked around and everything seemed so grim, yet there was something about his truck that was neat. Organized even. Maybe he knew his own mess. "Well what do you want with me?"

"Before we get into all of that, is that your titty?" His long finger pointed at my lap and when I looked down I saw the white sock that was supposed to be my breast nestled in my lap. Embarrassed, I quickly picked it up and stuffed it inside my purse. Once I made sure the other one was still in my bra, I took it out and tossed it in my bag too. Clearing my throat I said, "It happens sometimes." I looked out the window. "Now what?"

"Listen, I know you don't want to hear this but I feel the need to be real with you. Not because I'm trying to be your father but because you're a black boy and I'm a black man."

"Stop with the fake shit." I said putting my hand in his face. "You made it clear how you felt about me and I'm okay with that."

He slapped my hand away and leaned closer. I could smell the garlic on his breath. "Listen, you little nigger. I know you use to talking to people like they less than human but I'm not the one." He paused. "You will respect me and in turn, if you earn it, I may learn to respect you too."

I rolled my eyes, still feeling the sting of his blow.

"Now you're right, I didn't come off the best way when dealing with you boys. It's just that I know this story, seen it all before and like I told you at the house, things won't end well."

I replayed in my mind how good Rico tasted before shaking my head. The last thing I wanted was to be having sexual thoughts with Toppy alone in the car. "What are you talking about now?"

He leaned back in his seat and the leather moaned. "I had a nephew, who was just like you. He went out in the world pretending to be female, and that's okay, 'cept he never told the dudes he was in contact with so they felt duped. I might seem like I'm gay bashing but that's not it. If you tell folks how you roll, and who you really are, then I have no problem with what you do. But somebody who didn't have the same sense of humor as me murdered him and it killed my sister. Broke her heart. And it will kill your mother too."

Now he had my attention.

"I love Stacy. I always have. But she's a white woman who has no idea about the struggle black boys face in America. If you want to do this, if you want to be this, then I support you whether I like it or not. But whatever you do don't let her drunk ass convince you that this is the only way. Live your truth, just as long as you don't trick other people out of theirs."

For the next five minutes we didn't say a word to each other on the way home. I was realizing that Toppy, for all the anger he possessed, actually cared. As I replayed his words in my mind I thought about Rico and how much I liked about him. He didn't deserve to be with me without knowing the whole truth. But how would I tell him?

When we pulled up in front of my house my Aunt Stacy was out front, standing in the doorway, holding a beer. "What we talked about, with my nephew, stays between us," he said before parking. "Your aunt is a sweet lady but she doesn't understand everything."

"Okay," I said softly. "And thank you again, I'll think about what you said."

We both hopped out of the truck. He walked up to her, kissed her on the cheek and disappeared inside.

I strolled up to her and said, "Hey, Auntie."

Instead of responding with love like she did him she slapped me in the face. Drunk as an Irishman on St. Patrick's Day she said, "I know what you doing, nigga!"

I held my warm face. Was I somewhere else? Or was I at my aunt's house, where I was supposed to be loved, only to be attacked? "What's going on? I'm confused!"

"No matter how many socks you stuff in your bra you will never be a woman, bitch! Ever! And that means you can never have my man! Some things in this house are just off limits."

By Paige Lohan

CHAPTER ELEVEN

JOE

My head throbbed and my mind wouldn't let me rest. All night I was thinking of Rico and would he still like me in the morning, especially after the way I left. If my thoughts weren't on him they were on Aunt Stacy and how she hit me in the face.

I never thought the day would come where she would accuse me of being with her boyfriend, something I would never do. I can't even understand why the thought would come to her head. First off Toppy has a face only she could love. Second I would never hurt my aunt in that way.

After getting dressed for school, I grabbed my Neverful LV bag and walked toward my door when Aunt Stacy covered it with her body, preventing me from walking around her. Her chin was dipped toward her chest and she was playing with the belt on her pink robe. "You know I'm sorry." She looked up at me. "Right, honey? You know I would, or could never think of you in that way. Right?"

I looked down at the floor and crossed my arms over my body. I bit my bottom lip and said, "It's obvious you do think of me that way. Why else would you accuse me of something so wicked? Like where would that even come from?"

"It was the alcohol."

"It's always the alcohol with you, and people forgive you all the time. Well I'm not feeling the games no more so if you will excuse me." I tried to walk around her and she stepped in front of me again.

"I have a jealousy problem, especially when I have to live with two people who are more attractive than me."

"Stop playing, you know you're beautiful."

"And I'm also fat," She snapped. "Men get tired of seeing women who let their bodies flop. And I guess I'm worried that seeing you girls day in and day out will make him think about getting someone a little better than me." She touched my arm. "I'm sorry, Joe, I truly am, do you forgive me?"

"Yes," I said dryly.

"I want to hear you say it," she persisted, squeezing my arm a little. She claimed it was the alcohol that caused her to accuse me of fucking her man but I could smell liquor on her skin right now. Was that the only reason she was apologizing?

"I said I'm fine."

"Well I won't be able to stand myself if I don't hear the words, Joe. You have no idea how terrible I feel right now."

I looked into her eyes. "Is it as terrible as I felt when you forced me to dress like a girl and then accused me of getting up with your man?"

She exhaled, and her breath was stronger. A cross between garlic and booze. "I'm sorry, Joanne. You're...you're right. I wasn't thinking."

"Joe," I said correcting her. "At school I'll play the game but so you won't forget, around here I'm going by my birth name." I rolled my eyes, pushed her out of the way and walked out.

When I made it outside I was surprised to see Luke sitting on the porch. Canyetta had been picking him up but I guess after last night she may have blamed him for not convincing me to stay away from Rico. Like he had the authority.

When he saw me he got up and we headed toward school, not talking to each other for five minutes. Feeling like a hypocrite for sucking Rico off after I called him out on his shit for going upstairs with Thomas, I looked over at him. "You look pretty today."

He laughed and continued to walk.

"You were right about them jeans, they fit you way better than they did me. I could've never rocked them—"

"Is that your way of apologizing, honey?" he paused. "Because if it is you doing a fucked up job."

I laughed a little and shook my head. "I'm sorry."

"And what exactly are you sorry about?"

"For everything," I said throwing my hands up in the air. "For making a big deal when you went upstairs with Thomas, to not believing you were raped by Marcus. And for throwing what happened with your father in your face. It was wrong and if my mother was here she'd never forgive me."

"Bullshit, I know you never liked me, Joe."

"That's not true, I love—"

He threw his hand up. "Cut the shit. I know the 'T' so ain't no use in lying. You never liked me and I get why. What you don't know is that I always looked up to you. I admire how you never seemed to need a soul when I couldn't spend five minutes by myself without going mad."

It was hard taking credit for something I didn't do on purpose. I was a loaner because unlike Luke nobody fucked with me. "I wish I had your life," I admitted.

"Why, because of all the dick I get?" he joked.

I frowned. "No, bitch!" I laughed. "Because there's nothing braver than making yourself available for people, even when you know they may hurt you." I thought about Rico again and tried to get his face out of my mind. "Did you have sex that night? With Thomas?"

He nodded yes. "But it was trash anyway so I wouldn't recommend it."

I pulled my books closer to my chest, my chin resting on top of them. "But how, like, didn't he know?"

"At first he didn't, because of how I had my hands." He sighed deeply and shook his head. "I was getting too far into it and put my hands up, that's when he snaked his hand around my body and touched my penis."

I tried to conceal my anger but I knew this would happen. And then I thought about what I'd done to Rico so I had no room to judge. "Is that what happened to your eye? He hit you?"

He nodded yes. "Joe, I know it was wrong, that I did what I did but I detest fighting with my cousin. Not only are we blood, but we're also best friends. After everything we've gone through I feel like we should have each other's backs more."

I felt a dullness in my chest when I heard his words. "I know, and all I can say is you're right. I can't say things will be how they use to be but I'll try."

"With you not liking me that's the last thing I want. I mean for things to be the same," he said with a smile. "I think we should worry about getting to know each other, and respecting our differences."

I nodded and looked down at my books. "You think Thomas is gonna say something? About you being a boy?"

"Chile please," he waved at the air, not taking things serious as usual. "I told that nigga if he did I was going to shout to everybody that he was a big ole butch queen and loved every second of it. Trust me, the last thing he thinking about is opening that mouth

By Paige Lohan

about our personal business, honey." Luke must've felt I wasn't buying it because he grabbed one of my hands. "Trust, let me handle things. You don't have to worry."

I stopped walking and we hugged. "If you say you got it I believe you.

When we made it to the building we pulled open the doors and I noticed Thomas standing with Carlo, the craziest kid in our school. Thomas was staring in our direction and nothing about either of their looks was friendly to me. "You sure you got this nigga under control?" I asked. "Because the looks he's giving us right now are serious."

Luke laughed. "Girl bye, the last thing he gonna do is run that mouth. That's one thing I'm sure of."

THOMAS

Thomas and Carlo stood across the hallway staring at Joanne and Lolita as they entered the building. Carlo wasn't aware of what went on between his friend and Lolita; he was just wearing his naturally mean face.

As Lolita walked further inside, Thomas's extremities seemed to vibrate. His neck was corded and his hands were clenched tightly. Ever since Lolita tricked him into having sex he had nightmares about the day, often dreaming of ways he could get revenge in his sleep.

Carlo, the school's resident psychopath, stood next to him high and drunk as usual. Peeping Joanne and Lolita he said, "I can't believe you fucked that bad bitch. She ain't got a body like the other one but that face so pretty." He gripped his dick and eyed Lolita as she walked by. "If I ever get a chance to tap that I'ma show and prove. I hope you don't mind, fam, but I been plotting on that pussy from day one."

Thomas planted his feet wide apart and looked over at him. "Shut up, nigga. The last thing you want to do is fuck that bitch, trust me."

He frowned. "What's wrong with you?" Carlo's eyes widened with confusion. He scratched his scalp. "You bagged a good thing and you mad about it? Or is it because I said I wanted to tap that too? I hope you not mad about that fam, I was just fucking around."

"I don't care what you do with that bitch. Me bagging her was the worst thing that could've happened." He looked at Joanne and Lolita again who were now at their lockers across from him. "It was the worst thing that could've happened to you too."

"Me?" Carlo pointed to himself. "How you figure?"

"Look at that bitch again, take a good look and tell me what you see."

Carlo complied and was staring so hard people looked at him crazily. "What am I looking at?"

"Don't that bitch look old as fuck?"

He shrugged. "Not really."

"Well she is," Thomas snapped. "And the reason is she's an undercover cop." He blinked a few times, thinking of his lies as he went along. "So while you smiling over there, know that the bitch is here to lock us up."

Carlo placed his fingers on his stomach and looked like he was about to be ill. Dropping his hands by his sides he leaned up against the locker. "When did you figure this shit out?" he whispered. "And why you just telling me?"

"I saw something that looked like a badge in her purse, after I fucked her. It was shiny and it stood out to me at that time. I just needed to make sure so I asked around. Plus who comes to school in the middle of the year? I should've known then things were strange."

"People who move from other states."

"Stop being stupid!" Thomas snapped. "I may have believed that if it wasn't for the badge, but I'm telling you what I saw. And if we don't do something about it we gonna go down. You got ten to fifteen years in you, because I don't?"

Carlo nervously rubbed his Mohawk. "I don't want to get locked up."

"So what you willing to do to stop it from happening?" Thomas asked staring directly into his eyes. "Because me, I'm willing to do anything." He pointed at his chest.

As Thomas watched his friend come to terms with his lies he felt better already. He knew the things Carlo was capable of once he was unleashed.

Thomas didn't think of the cop story until the moment Lolita and Joanne walked into school. There was no way he could allow Lolita to get away with deceiving him but he couldn't call him out either. If people thought he was gay his social life would be dead.

Carlo's eyes looked liked they were crossed as he thought about the things he could do to Lolita and the way he could do it. "On everything I love, I'm willing to do anything. Even kill."

CHAPTER TWELVE

CANYETTA

C anyetta, Thomas and Carlo sat at a wooden table in her house, eating some thawed out microwave hamburgers that her mother bought the night before. Like most of the kids in the neighborhood, Canyetta was charged with taking care of herself, although her mother tried to make up for her absence by buying her a used truck and spoiling her rotten.

When the meal was done Canyetta grabbed the last napkin on the table, wiped her mouth and looked at them. She leaned back in her chair, crossed her legs and lowered her brows. "Now that the meal is done stop fucking around and tell me what you want?"

Carlo laughed. "Whoa, cousin, you act like you don't have no love for me no more."

"First off you haven't been at my house in months. And when I tried to buy a bag from you that day I realized it was dried grass instead of weed. Forgot about that shit?"

He pointed at her playfully. "But I got you back on the next one didn't I? Gave you more for the buck and everything."

"I'm serious, Carlo!" she hit the table. "I don't fuck with you which is why I'm surprised you even at my house. Talking about how much you miss your auntie and shit. Then you slide by here when you know she at work so you wouldn't have to see her. My mother may have got excited when you told her you would stay tonight for dinner but I didn't. Now what the fuck is up, before I put you both out?"

Thomas looked at Carlo and back at her. Taking a deep breath he said, "It's about Lolita."

She shrugged and popped the lid to a Coke. "What about the bitch?"

"So I take it you don't like her either?" Thomas said.

"It ain't about liking her." She took a big gulp and slammed it down. It was clear she was annoyed and holding her feelings back. "It's about not giving a fuck if the bitch lives or dies."

Carlo nodded. "Well we think she's police," He said. "And if she is it causes a problem for us. I already got a juvie record and if they get me for something else I'm facing adult time. I can't have that if you know what I'm saying."

Canyetta threw her head back and busted out into hysterical laughter. Holding her stomach it seemed like forever for her to calm down, while Thomas and Carlo watched. "Even if it was true, how you figure she's a cop? I mean look how young she is."

"They recruit the young faced ones early," Carlo said. "This not a game."

"Plus I saw her badge at the party," Thomas said pointing at the table.

She stopped laughing and looked at them seriously. "Was she a cop before or after you fucked her?" she laughed. "I didn't go to the party but – "

"You didn't come because Rico was there and Carlo said you didn't want to see him," Thomas said cutting her off.

"It doesn't matter, I may not have gone but I heard you were pressed for that pussy. Even acted like you didn't want nobody else to get it, and played her close all night. Now after all of this time she's a cop? Get the fuck out of here."

"It's not funny," Thomas said as he glared at her. "What I got to lie for?"

"I don't know, nigga, you tell me."

Thomas tapped Carlo on the shoulder. "Let's roll, she ain't feeling us." He stood up.

"Wait a minute," Carlo said looking up at him. "We need her."

She crossed her arms over her chest and witnessed Thomas take his seat again. "If she is a cop I will say this, she's doing a lot to get her man because I don't know too many of 'em who will fuck the same people she trying to arrest," She continued. "Plus it ain't even like ya'll moving major weight. Coming to Daniel High off the strength of you two niggas would be dumb and a complete waste of time."

Carlo felt insulted. "We are moving weight. Just because you got grass that one time don't mean it's different."

She waved them off. "Bitches, please, ya'll barely making ends meet. Didn't you have to borrow five dollars from me for lunch the other day, Carlo? That you still didn't give back?"

Carlo cleared his throat. "I didn't want to break my fifty."

"Cut the shit! Ya'll just not that big of a target. If she's a cop something else is up, but it don't have shit to do with drugs."

Thomas brought his fist down on the table so hard everything on the edge fell to the floor, and that included three plastic plates and her soda. "I'm not fucking around, Canyetta! Get serious before I do!"

Realizing the joke was over she swallowed and said, "I'm just messing around." She readjusted in her seat. "No need to get so ridiculous." She cleared her throat and placed her hands in her lap. "So what you want from me?"

"We want you to try and convince Lolita to come to your house, this weekend, when auntie go to Vegas," Carlo said. "We need to rap to her a little, in private. To see if it is true."

She looked at Carlo and then Thomas. Releasing the top button on her shirt she said, "I can probably do that...but if I do then what's gonna happen?"

"Then I'm gonna try and get the truth out of her, with a little force if I have too," Carlo said.

She leaned forward, clasped her hands on the table and looked at Carlo. "I'll do it on one condition."

"What's that?" Thomas asked.

"That you include Joanne too, and I want her to have the same treatment."

Thomas looked at Carlo and back at her. "Done."

Lolita was lying on his bed face up when he ended the call with Canyetta. He hopped off of the bed and quickly moved to Joanne's room. "Who are the most popular bitches in the school? Already?"

Joanne was sitting on the floor playing with a deck of cards. "Let me guess...you and you?"

Lolita jumped around the room playfully. "I'm serious!"

Joanne placed the cards down and looked up at her. "Okay, I know what you want me to say so here it is. Me and you?"

"Yessss, bitch! And guess who was invited to another party this weekend?"

Not feeling like playing games she sighed and said, "Us?" The last thing she felt like doing was going to a party.

"Indeed!" Lolita sat on the floor across from her. "And this party is supposed to be like that. Canyetta is having something small and some college boys are going to be there. Catered...liquor and weed on deck! The only thing I need is you."

"You want me to believe that Canyetta invited me to her house?" Joanne pointed at herself.

"Girl, I didn't believe it at first either but it's true. I started to call your ass in my room and put her on three way, it was so crazy."

Joanne rolled her eyes. "Come on, Luke, I don't know what she said to you on that phone but if she invited me it's

By Paige Lohan

not a good look. The last time I saw her I was at Rico's house and she was thrown out because he was with me. And did you see her face last week?"

"Her swollen nose?"

"Yes, that was all my work."

Lolita shoved her playfully. "What the fuck? Why didn't you tell me? That's why that bitch stopped talking to me. It makes so much sense now."

"Because it was too much drama. Just know that she was so mad she got in her truck and fired a gun into the air. Plus I'm not feeling like hanging out this weekend. Let's stay home, order a pizza and watch some movies."

Lolita pouted. "Honey, I am not a golden girl. You always so fucking boring." She stood up and sat on Joanne's bed, crossing her arms over her chest. "But she said she really wanted you to come. I felt like if you don't she doesn't want me either."

"And that gives me the creeps, Luke. Please don't go."

"You know I can't do that, I'm a wild child."

"I think she's trying to set me up," Joanne said seriously. "Especially if she invited me."

Lolita seemed anxious. She popped up and said, "Okay this is what I'll do. I'll go to the party and when she *ask where you are I'll just say you're on your way. That way I can scope things out and see what's going on."*

"And I'm asking you to stay," Joanne persisted. "This just doesn't sound right."

Luke walked up to her, sat next to her and grabbed her hands. "I know this girl thing is going to be over after school, and I'll be a boy again. But for now I want to live it to its limits. And whether you go or not all I'm asking is that you support me. Okay?"

Joanne believed in her heart that something was off but she was done fighting with her cousin. Besides if something was going on with Canyetta Joanne believed she was the real target, not Luke. So her cousin should be safe. "Okay, you like it I love it. Have fun." She kissed her on the cheek.

CHAPTER THIRTEEN

JOE

Dinner was served—fries, fried chicken and homemade lemonade. I just placed the serving plates on the table and was heading to Luke's room to tell him to come eat when Aunt Stacy walked into the kitchen, looking a mess as usual. Things had gotten weird between us since she accused me of sleeping with Toppy, and although I tried to wear a smile as I passed her in the hall, it was obvious that things were different.

"Everything looks good, Joanne," she said eyeing the plates. As if she remembered my request to be called by my government while home she shook her head and said, "I mean, Joe."

I walked over to the sink and washed my hands, wiping them dry on the red towel over my shoulder. "Thank you, Auntie." I rolled my eyes, tiring of the phoniness around here.

She pulled out a chair and said, "Sit down. Talk to me for a minute. Things have been so bad with us that I just want to put it out in the air." She closed her robe tighter and crossed her pale legs. "That way we can be done with it."

I sighed under my breath. There's nothing worse than someone wanting to have a conversation when you don't feel like being bothered. "But the food's gonna get cold. Plus Luke keeps coming out here every five minutes asking if it's done. Can't we do this later? Or another day?"

"It won't take long," she said reaching up to touch my hand, pulling me softly toward the seat next to her. "I promise."

I sighed, pulled out the chair, sat down and crossed my arms over my chest. "Yes, Auntie?" My foot jiggled briskly.

"I know I told you I'm sorry for reacting the way that I did, but I don't believe that you really understand how much."

"It's okay, I'm not even —"

"Let me talk, Joe. Please." She placed her hand up, which was so close to me it almost touched my nose. "Like I said, I know you accepted my apology but I need you to understand why I really feel awful." She dropped her hand. "For the past few years, since my daughters were killed, I never told a soul what really happened. What led up to it, the accident. People in the family speculated but nobody really knew what happened."

I sat up, trying to resist the urge that I was finally about to hear some deep family secret. "I'm listening."

"I've always had a taste for strong liquor, but when I was betrayed in the worst ways I took to the bottle even harder. That's when my real troubles began."

My eyebrows rose. "Who betrayed you?"

I could tell she didn't want to say it. Her mouth opened and closed. "Monroe and your mother."

I couldn't move left or right. My body felt stiff, like all of my organs had shut down. When I tried to talk my tongue felt weighted and I was also having trouble breathing. After calming down a few seconds I looked into her eyes, "Are you trying to say that my mother and your husband, her brother-in-law, had an affair?"

"Don't be so surprised, things happen when you're grieving, and your mother was grieving hard when my brother died on that boat. It was so bad that she could barely take care of herself."

She acted as if I wasn't there experiencing it first hand. I was the one who had to clean her when she couldn't do it. "The three of us were close before my father died, of course it hurt my mother." My tone was slightly defensive but I felt it needed to be because there was no way I was coming to terms that the sweetest woman I ever knew could be foul.

"To be honest I never blamed your mother. I knew where the responsibility lied, with my husband. It made no sense that he would fly all the way from Baltimore to North Carolina, repeatedly to see a woman he didn't have a strong relationship with. That was my brother's wife, not his friend."

My mind went back to the days we would drive to the airport and pick up Uncle Monroe. I remember those times being the happiest moments of my life after my father died, because my mother seemed so inspired. So happy. Now I guess I know why.

"Monroe thought I didn't know but I was on to him the moment it happened. He smelled different when he came back, and wouldn't touch me for a few days at a time. The twins would always ask what was wrong with their father when he returned, and I never

By Paige Lohan

wanted to get them involved. I wanted their thoughts of their father to remain pure...until he did the ultimate."

She stopped talking and my heart pounded. Placing my hand over top of hers I said, "What happened?"

Her eyes widened and she looked at me as if she were reliving the moment all over again. "He said he was leaving me for her. Said he wanted a divorce."

"But...mama...she would never do that. She loves you too much." I shook my head in disbelief, feeling myself sweating lightly on my forehead. "Plus she was big on marriage. You must've misunderstood."

"I would never misunderstand something like that!" she said through clenched teeth. "I'm telling you that he wanted out of our marriage because it's true." She grew quiet again and her tense body appeared to relax. She looked up at the ceiling and clasped her hands in her lap. "All I wanted was to take the girls for a ride, to get some fresh air. I had been drinking but I guess I didn't realize how much. It was snowing that day, the roads were really bad and suddenly I lost control of the car. I lost control of myself."

I didn't want to say anything but it was starting to sound like she killed my cousins on purpose, to get back at Uncle Monroe. "But it was an accident. You got the life insurance pay out and everything."

"We were in a ditch for three days before they found the car, Joe. All of the liquor was out my system by then. And my girls...my girls..." her cheeks bubbled up as she cried harder. "My girls were dead, in the car with me for all those days. There is no punishment they could've handed down that would be worse than that. To smell their flesh rotting, knowing it was my fault, killed my soul." She wiped her eyes. "Of course Monroe hung himself the next day, believing he was responsible and then your mother...well your mother turned to another addiction since my husband wasn't there anymore."

I stood up and looked down at her. "What you trying to say?" My body trembled because I couldn't take anymore.

"I'm sorry," she said with her palm, which was red like strawberries pointing at me. "Please sit."

I don't know what she was getting at but I didn't want to hear another bad thing about a woman I loved. First Luke tells me that my mother knew that auntie was going to kill her husband before she did it, and now this.

"What I really wanted to say was that I have some demons. Many of them. And I haven't been my best, which is why a few days ago I enrolled in A.A. I'm taking my life back and I wanted you to know it was because of what happened that day. When I hit you. You are my flesh and blood, the only blood I have left from my brother and I don't want to lose you."

I was so proud of her I stood up and hugged her before sitting back down. Temporarily forgetting all of the bad things she said. "You don't know how good it feels to hear you say that because I...well...I want to take my life back too."

She wiped her tears with her knuckles. "What do you mean?"

I cleared my throat. "I'm thinking about telling the truth about my identity. To Rico. And the people at school."

Her eyes widened. "Joe, please don't do that." She placed her wet hand over mine. "I know how children are and it will be difficult for you at school. I'm begging you to reconsider."

"Aunt Stacy, I've already made my decision. I can't be this other thing anymore. I can't lie just so I won't have to deal with the issues that surround it. I'm gay, and it's the cross I have to bear. But I think I'm finally ready."

The Next Day

My mother was sitting in her favorite rocking chair, on the patio of her house. The sun was brilliant orange and a comfortable breeze surrounded us. Although she still looked frail there was something different about her. It was like she really came to terms with dying, and was actually looking forward to it. Her peace broke my heart.

"Do you know I prayed for you to be born," she said gazing over at me before looking ahead again. "And you're not going to believe this but I even think I had a hand in you being gay."

"Mama," I laughed tapping her arm playfully. "Who in the world prays for a gay black son?"

By Paige Lohan

"I'm serious." She nodded. "I prayed that you would be kind, sweet and have a fashion flair. Remember back in the day, after your daddy died, I ran the women's department at Nordstrom's. Style was important to me." She ran her hand down her light blue muumuu and struck a seated pose. "It still is now you just can't tell."

I laughed harder. "I could not have thanked God for a better mother." I touched her hand and squeezed lightly. She looked at me. "I really mean that."

"Then we are more alike than I thought." She paused. Her voice grew more serious. "Now, son, tell me what's wrong? What would make you fly out here on a Friday? You should be having fun, with friends."

I exhaled. "Aunt Stacy told me something, about you and —"

"It's true, baby, all true," she said looking out ahead. "And I'm ashamed of my mistakes and if I'm being honest, I was hoping she would tell you. I guess I was too cowardly to do it myself, but leave it to your aunt to do it for me." She laughed. "Was she drunk when she told you?"

Still stunned by hearing auntie was right about the affair, I tried to smile, but I was filled with shame.

Shame that mama would hurt someone when she knew what it felt like to lose a husband. "No, she's actually going to A.A. She says she's changing her life now."

She looked at me in disbelief. "Well, good, good for her." She sounded sincerely happy. "Joe, I never want to feel that kind of grief again. The kind that would turn you selfish and numb to anyone else's feelings; especially someone you love. I turned to coke after Monroe killed himself. For two whole weeks and then I stopped cold turkey."

"Why drugs?" I asked almost trembling. "Why would you do that?"

"When you experience hurt that great you just want to feel." She touched her arms. "And then one day, after buying a bag of coke I came home and you decorated the entire house. The kindness...it lifted me."

I smiled. "I remember that day, didn't know why you were so sad."

"You said it was a party and that we were celebrating our new lives together. That was the turning point for me, Joe, and I haven't touched it since."

Only my mama could make me ashamed and proud in the same minute. I turned my chair toward her. "Mama, I have to tell the truth about something and I'm afraid if I do it will hurt someone I care about."

She nodded. "I know a lot about that. Hurting people that is." She laughed softly. Well, son, if you don't tell the truth, will you be able to live with yourself? Will you embrace each day with your head up, knowing that you were living your fullest life?"

"No…"

"Then you already know what needs to be done."

"But what about hurting that someone?"

"If you really care about this person you should pull him or her to the side first. Let them know how you feel but you can't live with a lie another day. If they care about you, and accept your truth, then you've chosen wisely. If not you've been given the gift of never having to spend another day with someone who doesn't deserve you. Only the strongest can make the big decisions, son, and I think you're one of them."

Feeling vindicated I hugged her tightly. "Thank you, mama."

She kissed my cheek. "No, son, thank you."

When my cell phone rang I removed it from my pocket and answered. "Hello…"

"Joe, is Luke with you in North Carolina?" Aunt Stacy asked.

She sounded hysterical and that made me immediately nervous. "No, why, what's wrong?"

"I don't know. He hasn't been home all night and I'm worried sick. Something doesn't feel right."

By Paige Lohan

CHAPTER FOURTEEN

CARLO

*L*olita stood in the corner, covered in her own bodily waste as Carlo stood before her, holding a knife dripping in blood. She was naked from the waist down. "Please don't do this," she pleaded, barely able to stand. No longer having the strength her knees buckled and she slid to the floor. "I'm sorry...I...I was...wrong. But please don't kill me." Her hands were outstretched, her fingertips trembled.

"You're a fuckin' faggy!" Carlo yelled looking down. His face held so many frown lines he looked twenty years older. "You walked around school, faking like a bitch and the whole time..." His words disappeared and he found himself consumed with more rage.

Although Carlo was never supposed to have sex with Lolita, alone in her presence he allowed his hormones to take over. Just looking at her petite body, her doe shape eyes and her smile had him wanting a taste of what Thomas had. Just like Joe her bone structure was feminine, and he looked nothing like a boy.

Two seconds in the rape, it wasn't long before he discovered that she was a he.

"I'll do anything, Carlo," she sobbed. "Anything, just please don't take me away from my family, away from my cousin."

Carlo wasn't receiving anything Lolita was saying. He was confused, thoughts heavy on his mind about what was the truth verses a lie played on repeat. "I can't believe you out there faking, I mean are you even a cop?" He lowered his body and stabbed her again in the chest. Carlo wasn't a seventeen-year-old misguided teen; in the moment he was a madman with no sense of value for life.

Lolita sat in the corner with one hand outstretched; it was all she could hold out. Blood covered her tongue and she could feel herself slipping away. "I don't...know what you want me to say...I'm sorry." Her head dropped back into the wall, her body sloped to the side.

"Are you a fucking cop or not?" he yelled.

"No," was the last thing she said before she slipped away.

When Carlo heard loud banging at the front door he threw the knife in the corner and rushed toward it, pulling it open he was out of breath, as if he ran a 5K. Thomas rushed inside, slamming the door behind himself. "Why you bring her to your house?"

Carlo's jaw twitched. "Her huh?"

By Paige Lohan

"What?" Thomas said, unaware of his stiff mood. "I went to your cousin's house and she said you brought her here. Why?"

Instead of being warm Carlo laid into him. "Why you ain't tell me the bitch was a nigga! Huh? Why you ain't tell me you fucked a dude?"

The smile wiped clean off Thomas's face. "I don't know what you talking about." His chin dipped downward and he stuffed his hands in his pockets. "Stop fucking around and tell me where the bitch at."

Carlo stepped closer and stuck a stiff finger into his chest. "You told me you fucked the bitch! Remember? The night of the party. So why you faking dumb now?" His nostrils flared so wide you could put an orange through each. "Is it, or is it not a man?"

Thomas, realizing he was caught, walked over to the sofa and sat on the arm. He now saw her body in the corner and sighed. Things were so messy. He wiped is hands down his face. "Even if I did fuck her how would you know? The only thing you were supposed to do was hold her until I got to your cousin's house. And what do you do? Bring her here!" he pointed at her. "Now you coming at me about some other stuff that don't have nothing to do with business?"

Carlo walked away and leaned up against the wall. "I know you knew this shit, man. I know you knew it was a dude. So keep it real with me."

Thomas stood up and circled the space in front of the sofa. When he was ready he took a deep breath and looked at his friend. "Even if it was true we can't let nobody find out. You know what we gotta do."

Carlo took a deep breath. "Yeah, dump her."

What Happened Earlier

Lolita stepped out of the cab, alone, dressed to kill. Wearing a pair of new designer blue jeans, she completed her look with a form-fitting top and carried her new white LV bag. Already buzzed, she was eager to see what the night held in store. Her only sadness came from not being with Joanne who she felt needed to come along and loosen up. But she wasn't about to let her ruin the night either.

After paying the cab driver she knocked on Canyetta's door but the first person she saw caused her extreme irritation. "What are you doing here, Carlo?" she asked leaning against the doorframe. "And why is it so quiet inside? I thought we were supposed to be turning up?"

Carlo smiled. "The party's been moved to another spot." He closed the door behind himself and walked toward his black Honda. He deactivated the alarm and looked behind himself when he didn't hear her walking. "Coming or not?"

Lolita shrugged. "What the fuck, I ain't doing nothing else."

She slid inside his car and she was so twisted she passed out sleep. Within fifteen minutes she was inside of his dirty, dark apartment, sitting on the sofa. Taking a look around she said, "What time is everything supposed to be going down?"

Carlo locked the door, pushed some dirty laundry off of the other end of the couch and sat down. "Actually they coming in about thirty minutes." He looked at his watch.

"Well, if I got to sit in here I don't want my buzz ruined." She leaned back and looked over at him. "You got something to drink in this bitch?"

"Yeah, sure, what you want?"

"The strongest thing you got because I can see this party is already about to blow me." She closed her eyes and opened them again. "Had I known it was gonna be like this I would've never came."

Carlo hopped up and prepared a concoction of a cheap sweet strawberry cooler and Hennessey. He handed her the large styrophone cup and sat next to her again, this time a little closer. "So your friend not coming?"

"She's my cousin and she said she might come later." She gulped down half of the liquor, opened her thighs and sat the cool cup between her legs. "Now I'm gonna have to give her the new address." She reached in her purse and grabbed her cell.

"Wait," he yelled, startling Lolita. "I mean, wait until everybody gets here."

She nodded, and put it back in her purse. It wasn't like Joanne was coming anyway.

"So why you not fucking with my man no more?"

"Who's your man?"

"Now you gonna play games?"

Lolita sighed. "Listen, all I want to do is get some drinks and chill. The last thing on my mind is Thomas or you for that matter." She looked around again. "As a matter of fact I'm gonna leave and come back later. Can you call me a cab?"

"Come on, ma, stop playing games and give me some of that pussy." He was done with being nice and moved to place his hand over Lolita's crotch when she pushed it away and stood up.

"What the fuck is wrong with you?" she screamed. "Why you coming at me all hard?" she clutched her purse to her chest. "Just let me go home."

He rushed toward her, his mood anxious. "Why you playing games, huh? Thomas already told me how good that pussy is."

Lolita was fussing with the door until he said those words. Slowly she turned around and looked at him before breaking out into laughter. "Oh yeah? Tell me how good it was. Tell me how wet it was and don't leave out a thing he said."

Carlo's dick grew harder, thinking she was getting turned on. "He said it was juicy, wet and pretty too." Having lied his face off, he placed a hand each on her hips. "And that you smell good down there and all I want is a sniff."

Instead of enjoying the compliment Lolita's laughter grew more intense. "He said all that huh?"

"What's so funny?"

"Let me tell you why I know it's not true, because he never smelled my pussy, and never will." She looked around again. "There probably ain't even no party here tonight is

A School of Dolls   153

it?" he paused. "All this was a set up to fuck me." She tried to leave again when Carlo knocked her in the face with a closed fist.

Attempting to stand, she was struck again before being kicked in the stomach. She was face down, trying to cough air back into her lungs. On the floor and partially unconscious, Carlo dropped down with her, and pulled Lolita's pants to her knees. He quickly undid his own.

Like a rabid dog, salivating for food, he pushed Lolita's cheeks apart and rammed his penis into her anus. When it started feeling good, he reached around and felt for her vagina, touching her penis instead.

Disgust overwhelmed him although he hadn't bothered to pull out. He almost reached and orgasm and continued to push into Lolita's limp body, as he felt his nut coming along. Once he was done, he ejaculated on Luke's buttocks, scooted toward the corner of the living room and threw up on the floor.

By Paige Lohan

CHAPTER FIFTEEN

JOE

I sat in the living room, on the sofa, looking at the TV, which was turned off. The house phone rang off the hook and I was too angry to pick it up. Yesterday they found my cousin's body in a dumpster behind a liquor store and my mind was in circles. All of the bad things I said to him and now this.

The cops had questions. My friends at school had questions. My family had questions and the only thing I wondered was why? Why would someone take the only person other than my mother who cared about me? And I realized that thought was selfish. It wasn't about me it was about Luke.

When the front door opened Aunt Stacy pushed herself inside. She looked sick, her pale skin splotched with red spots. Not drinking was taking a toll on her body. "I told her, honey. I told her what happened so you don't have to."

I exhaled and sat up straight. I felt like a coward for not telling my mother about Luke myself but I couldn't look into her eyes. "How did she take it?" I rubbed my forehead. "I mean, was she okay?"

She sat on the sofa next to me, her warm thigh against mine. "You were right, she took it hard." She placed her hand on my knee. "But you can't carry the weight of that, Joe. It wasn't your fault."

I shook my head, not wanting to listen. "My mother suffered more death than anyone I know."

"I lost my girls, and my husband." She sat back and folded her arms over her chest. "If you ask me we're neck and neck."

"I'm sorry, I didn't mean it that way. It's just—"

"I know, I know, just telling you how I feel that's all." She sighed and looked out into the living room as if she were about to cry. "Your mother is strong, Joe, she'll come around. You just have to give her some time that's all."

I don't know what it was but as I looked at her face I felt she bared more responsibility for Luke's death than anyone. Although I'm not sure if the murder was related to the identity change she forced us to make, I feel like if we never moved here my cousin would still be alive. "My mother has taken care of him for years, and even before that she loved him." I positioned my body so that I could stare directly into her eyes. "Luke doesn't have some cold, he's fucking dead! So she has a right to be upset!"

"Joe—"

"Joe nothing! You too lax when it comes to your part in all of this! How we know Luke didn't die because somebody found out about him? And you told my mother he was dead because you feel guilty, not because you care!"

Her eyes widened. "This is not fair, Joe." Her face was so red I thought all of her blood had rushed to her head. "Yes, I know it probably wasn't the best thing in the world to tell you guys to be who you weren't, but don't sit in my house and act like there wasn't a reason!"

I stood up and looked down at her, crossing my arms over my chest. "And what was that reason again?" I yelled. "Because I thought it was so we would be safe, and if that's the case please tell me why my cousin is dead!" I screamed in her face.

"Maybe you're right", she stated. "Toppy told me I was being ridiculous by making you boys be girls but I couldn't see it until then. I think part of me was genuine and was trying to protect you. But deep down

I think I was being selfish and was somehow trying to channel my girls through you two." She confessed.

She stood up and stood before me. "But the bottom line is all I wanted was to give you the best chance. And if you get upset about that then I got to take it, but if I had it to do all over again I probably would."

"Well I'm gad you don't because if it was up to you I would probably be dead too, bitch!" I stormed away.

FIVE DAYS LATER

This was the day I dreaded. Monday morning where I would have to go back to school and pass other kids who all wanted to know what happened to my cousin. I don't know how my Aunt Stacy did it but some way she was able to keep the sex of my cousin out of the newspaper. Instead of saying a young man was killed, it said a young teenager was found murdered. While I appreciated whatever needed to be done to keep Luke's business private, it didn't make me feel any better.

158   By Paige Lohan

Something was off and I wondered what I missed. I kept replaying in my head the party Luke was supposed to go to over Canyetta's house. I even gave them her name. When they questioned her and asked her had she seen him she said no, and that the party had been cancelled. Far as I know Canyetta wasn't close to Thomas so there wasn't a reason to lie.

Even Thomas was questioned. He said he didn't like her but didn't have any reason to kill her either. From what I'm told they were considering everybody and Thomas, although not charged, was still a suspect.

After taking my book out of my locker I turned around and Rico was standing in front of me. My legs felt weak as I looked at him because I forgot how much I liked him. Pulling my books closer to my sock stuffed chest I smiled and said, "Hey, Rico."

He placed one hand on the locker behind me, and stood so close I could kiss him if I wanted. "You a hard girl to catch. I was starting to think you hated me or something."

I looked down the hall at fat Kisha with the cute face, just to do something else with my eyes. "Hate you? What for?"

"I don't know, my cousin is being questioned and I didn't know if you blamed me."

"You know I don't."

"Well I been calling your house non-stop, Joanne." His brows lowered. "And I know we haven't made anything official but until another nigga step up I feel responsible for you."

I looked at him and then away again. "You shouldn't worry about me, I have my aunt and my mother so I'm never alone." I moved out of his direct path and he positioned his body so he could be in front of me again.

"I can't imagine what you going through right now. I fucked with Lolita too even though we didn't get a chance to really kick it. She wasn't as close as we are but she was still cool." He paused and lifted my chin, which had pointed downward. "All I'm asking is that you don't shut me out. Everybody needs someone, even you."

"Rico, I just need a little time by myself to figure—"

He kissed me. It was a long kiss, the kind that seemed to stop time, making us the only two people in the world. Instead of backing away I found myself kissing him back. I got so into it that I released the books in my arms, and could feel the soft thud of them dropping on my sandals. I wasn't sure but something told me I was falling in love.

Slowly he separated from me and the few kids around us started clapping. Everyone seemed happy for us, well, everyone except Canyetta. I didn't even know she was standing there. The moment my eyes met hers she stomped down the hallway and I knew before long we would see each other again.

Rico bent down and picked up my books, just as our audience went about their way. "That was nice, sexy." He paused and handed me my textbooks. "Can you come by my house later? I want to talk to you about some things."

I swallowed. "Me? For what?"

"I'll tell you when I see you," he smiled brighter. "Just promise me you're going to come."

I nodded even though I should've said no.

"Good, beautiful." He kissed me again, this time on the cheek. "I'll see you later."

The police arrested Thomas for the murder of my cousin and everybody in school was talking about it. Apparently he left some of his DNA behind, some hair I think, and they tested it before a warrant was issued for his arrest. There was more DNA but they couldn't find whom it belonged too. When word got out that it could be Carlo they went to find him but he was not home.

I felt heavy when I walked into my house after hearing the news. Aunt Stacy called the school and said I could come home early but I stayed. I needed to be around someone else because lately she was draining.

When I was inside the house I headed straight for the kitchen. I bypassed lunch earlier at school so I wouldn't have to hear a thousand questions about what happened to Luke, and now I was starved. I removed my wig, stuffed it in my book bag and exhaled. The air felt cool on my scalp.

Instead of grabbing something to eat the moment I stepped inside of the kitchen my appetite was gone. "What are you doing, Aunt Stacy?" I observed a spread of alcohol that sat on the table in front of her. She had Hennessey, beer and a pack of More's Menthol.

With a lit cigarette between her fingers she plucked the ashes on the floor. "Leave me alone, Joe," she said, her voice slurring. "I got a lot on my mind." She picked up the cup and placed it to her lips. "The last thing I need is a child telling me what to do."

I moved closer and remained standing. "But you quit! You told me you were done with that stuff!"

"Well I lied," she shrugged. "Maybe that's what A.A. is about, lying."

I could feel my pressure rising and I felt myself wanting to be violent. My aunt has always been a drunk, but I really believed she wanted to change, if nothing else for Luke. Guess I was wrong. "You know what, I hope you choke on that shit and die. I'm done caring about you or what you do to yourself."

She picked up the cup and placed it against her lips. "Yeah, yeah, tell me something I don't already know."

In The Backyard

Canyetta's fingertips were pressed against the outside of the kitchen window as she peered inside of Stacy's house. She couldn't believe what she was seeing. Joanne, her classmate, was actually a boy. Her head shook side to side and she tried to blink a few times to be sure she was seeing correctly. But after a few minutes nothing changed, Joanne was male. How could she miss it?

Afraid about what this information meant for Rico she backed quickly away from the window, hopped the fence and walked up the block toward her car. Her feet couldn't move fast enough because there was one person she had to see, Rico. As far as she knew he wasn't gay and would never be with another boy. It was up to her to give him the newfound information.

She was about to get inside her car when Carlo pulled up alongside her. "Come here for a second."

Her stomach rolled when she saw his face. The entire world was looking for him because of Lolita's murder so what was he doing there? "Not now, Carlo," she said deactivating her car alarm. "I have to get to Rico's house."

"This is important, that nigga can wait," he said calmly. When she didn't move quickly enough he said, "Don't make me get out of this car and snatch you up, cuz."

By Paige Lohan

Canyetta rolled her eyes, dropped her keys in her pocket and stomped toward her cousin's car. "Pull up the street." She pointed up the block. "I don't want to be close to this house."

Carlo drove further then she wanted and she could feel her pressure rising. She knew what people were saying about him and she hoped the blood they shared would mean she'd be safe. "Now what's up?" she asked, positioning her body to look directly into his eyes.

"I think Joe may cause problems for me." He gripped the steering wheel so hard his knuckles whitened.

"Carlo, the police are searching for you, for questioning. You have to turn yourself in or it's gonna look suspicious. They called my mother looking for auntie too, but they can't find her."

"You know my mother's a drunk," he said through clenched teeth. "Here it is, I'm in trouble with the law and she can't pull her head up from under the bottle for one minute."

Canyetta's right leg shook. "So you just gonna go on the run forever? Because the longer it takes to find you the more responsible they gonna think you are. I mean, did you have something to do with it? The last thing I remembered was you and Thomas asking me to bring her to the house and — "

He reached out and grabbed her neck, holding it a little longer than he meant to. She clawed at his fingers and realizing he went too far, he let her go. *"I'm sorry, cuz, I just..."*

She hacked a few times to get air into her lungs. Rubbing her throat she said, *"I should punch you in your fucking face!"* Her eyes watered and she wiped them.

"I'm sorry, cuz!"

"No, what you are is crazy! If my mama knew you just did that she would kick your ass." She leaned back into the seat, trying to determine if she should run.

"Did you tell the police that we asked you to invite her over to your house? Along with Joanne?"

"No, I said I was having a party but I cancelled it. They don't even know you and Thomas planned to be there." She took a deep breath. *"Did you have something to do with it or not?"*

Slowly his head rotated toward her. *"Yes. But what really fucked me up was when I found out she was a dude."*

"What are you talking about? The newspapers said her name was Lolita."

"If you noticed they kept saying teenager. Nothing about her sex." He paused. *"But its gonna come out soon, won't no reporter hold back on that juicy detail for long."*

　　　By Paige Lohan

Lolita was a man? Could it be that Joanne and Lolita both were frauds? As her thoughts continued to swim she was suddenly more afraid of him admitting to murder. "So you, killed him?"

"Didn't the fuck I just tell you that?" he yelled slapping the steering wheel. "But it ain't about what happened it's about what's gonna happen. Now I been looking for you all day because we have to finish what the three of us started."

Her brows lowered. "We?" She pointed to herself.

"Yes. You were the one who helped us set him up remember? And had you got Joanne to come like we planned she'd be gone too. Thomas is stand up, and he not gonna say shit about what happened in prison. But if they start snooping around and find out about the plan to meet at your house, he going down and I'm going down too. Who you think is gonna be next?"

She rubbed her throbbing temples.

"Cuz, all I want to do is finish this shit, after that I'll turn myself in," he said. "But if you don't help me, I'll kill you and that bitch too, blood or not."

STACY

Stacy sat at the kitchen table stewing over how Joe treated her earlier. Although she was into black men, and had black children, she hated how people of color acted some times. In her opinion it was like they ruled the world. She was filled with racist hate which usually only happened when her drunken periods would last longer than usual.

When there was a knock at the door she grabbed her bottle of liquor, stood up and stumbled backwards into the refrigerator. It took a few moments to pull herself together and move toward the living room. Once there she opened the door and frowned when she saw the boy she warned Joe to stay away from — Rico. "What the fuck are you doing here?" she slurred before taking a large sip.

"I'm here to see, Joanne," he said respectfully. "I was expecting her at my crib but she didn't show. I mean, if it's a bad time I can come back." He was preparing to turn around but stopped briefly for her response.

"So you're the one who has Joe confused?" she asked wobbling. "The one she can't stop thinking about."

Rico smiled before growing serious, it felt good to know he'd been on Joanne's mind as much as she'd been on his. "I may be, but right now we're just friends."

"Is that right?" she laughed. "Because I know young men like you, and the last thing you're thinking about is friendship."

He rubbed his chin. "Maybe I should go."

Stacy opened the door wider. "No, come in, I'm sorry. I get so drunk some times I don't know what I'm saying." She paused. "Let me take you back to her room, I'm sure you two have lots to talk about."

CHAPTER SIXTEEN

JOE

I was lying in bed thinking about all of the things that had gone on in the last few days when my cell phone rang. I was about to throw it across the room but I sat up, placed my feet on the floor and grabbed the phone off the dresser. When I looked there was a number I didn't recognize. Hitting the answer button I pressed the phone against my ear and said, "Hello..."

"Hi, Joanne. It's me, Canyetta. Is this a bad time?"

I thought about what was going on and felt like hanging up without a response, but curiosity was winning. What did she want? "I'm good, but if you're calling me about Rico he's not here."

She laughed softly. "No, it's nothing like that. I'm calling to tell you that I'm sorry about Lolita, I mean, I know you and I weren't close but I feel like we could've been if things were different."

"By different do you mean if Rico didn't like me? Because there was nothing really going on between us."

"What about the kiss in the hallway today at school?"

She got me and I could hear her heavy breaths as she waited for an answer. "Yeah, sorry about that. It was unexpected."

"Anyway I was also calling to see if you wanted to talk. I'm sure you're with family but if you wanted to come kick it with somebody who was cool with Lolita, I'm with it."

I thought her offer was strange but to be honest she caught me at a good time. I wasn't ready to face my mother and my Aunt was a mess these days. If I went to Canyetta's house maybe I could also find out why Luke liked her so much. Maybe there was something I was missing. "I'm not sure, Canyetta. We really never kicked it and you were about to shoot me."

She laughed. "That's wasn't a gunshot, that was my tailpipe."

I laughed. "Oh...I still don't know."

"Are you sure, because I have fruity liquor?" she laughed. "Something to take off the edge."

I laughed. "You know what, I'll be there. What time is good for you?"

"What are you doing tomorrow, after school?"

"I guess coming to your house," I smiled, surprised I was doing it.

"Cool, well I'll see you then, and please don't change your mind. I'm looking forward to putting all this mess behind us. I'm tired of girls fighting over guys when they could care less."

Not sure we were fighting but I understood her point. "Okay, I'll see you then."

When I hung up I felt someone was looking at me and was shocked when I turned my head and saw Rico. What the fuck was he doing here and how did he get in? Luckily I had placed my wig back on earlier to curl it but there were other wigs sitting on the dresser. I relaxed when I realized that real girls wear wigs too. "Hey, what you doing here? I look a mess."

He smiled. "I don't think you can ever look a mess, but to answer your question your aunt let me in."

I'm starting to really hate that fat bitch. "Well, why are you here? I told you I was coming over, why didn't you wait?" I scratched my leg even though it didn't itch.

"Because I thought you wouldn't come. I was right wasn't I?" His eye contact was strong.

I stood up and walked toward the corner of my room, away from him. "We can't be like this, Rico." I looked down at my toes. "We can't be what you want. And I know you think I'm playing hard to get but it's not the case."

"Be like what?" he laughed. "You're single and I'm looking for a girl so what's the problem?" He licked his lips. "And the fact that you give me such a hard time makes me want you even more."

"I'm trying in the best way possible to be real with you, because I never want you to think that I lied, or tried to deceive you, Rico." I felt tears forming in my eyes and I tried to hold them back. "You have no idea how hard I've been battling with all this."

"You sure it's not because of my cousin, and what he did to Lolita? Because I'm done with him too."

"It's not that. If he's involved he'll get what he deserves."

He seemed to get serious and sat in the only chair in my room, next to my wigs. "Well it's obvious you want to tell me something, so stop fucking around and say it, baby. Because right now, based on our kiss today, I feel like you're feeling me the way I'm feeling you."

"I am feeling you, have been from the first day I saw you."

"So why the fucking games?"

"I'm not who you think I am." I sat on the edge of my bed so that I was directly across from him, but not close enough for him to touch me. "The reason I relocated here, with my aunt, was because me and Lolita were the victims of a hate crime at home."

His eyebrows rose. "For being black?"

"No, for being gay."

He laughed. "That's all you're worried about, because I don't have a problem with my chick liking other girls. Just as long as you stop that when we get together."

"No, Rico, I'm saying that I'm a...I'm a boy." I pointed at myself, not sure why.

His head tilted to the side and he leaned back in his chair. His mouth opened and closed like he was trying to understand it all. "Like a boy in the relationship?"

When I saw he wasn't getting it I explained everything, from the day Luke and me were jumped in the school cafeteria, to us moving here and my aunt suggesting that we change our sex. During each second of my explanation I saw hate cover him, growing thicker as time went by.

When I was done he was silent.

He stood up, slowly walked over and looked down at me. He reached out and I jumped but he snatched the wig off my head. He took a step back as if he was just seeing me for who I was. "So you're telling me that you're a...you're a...fucking guy? With hair and all that fucking makeup on your face?" he grabbed my cheek. "But your face, it's like a girl."

I nodded. "I'm a boy."

Before I knew it his fist slammed down against my mouth, splitting my lip. I could taste blood filling up in my mouth as it trickled down on my chin. "I'm sorry," I said as the tears fell harder. "I know you don't believe me, Rico but this was never my intent."

"Shut the fuck up!" he yelled, his palm close to my face. "Just stop your fucking lies because I can't take anymore." Fifteen seconds of hard silence passed. "You lucky I didn't just kill you." He looked at me with hate, his skin reddening and his eyes watering, before storming out.

RICO

School was in an hour and at first it seemed like Rico was not fazed by what Joanne told him the night before. He had intentions on getting up, getting dressed and sliding into his car to tackle the day. He told himself that he made a mistake and as far as he was concerned, he was done with all things Joanne, if that was even her real name.

He was almost out the door when suddenly he ran out of mental gas.

Standing in front of the mirror he looked at his reflection, trying desperately to understand who he was now that he'd been with Joanne. Since he allowed him to give him oral sex, and had the best orgasm of his life, did that make him gay?

"Son, what's wrong?" Valerie, Rico's mother asked as she walked through his door. "Ever since last night you've been out of it, you have me worried."

Rico turned toward her. "Am I a bad person, ma? And don't just say no because I'm your son, I really want to know the truth."

She walked further in the room and stood before him. Placing her cool hands on his face she looked into his eyes. "Son, you could never be a bad person." She squeezed his cheeks just a little tighter. "People make mistakes, we all do, but I know your heart." She took a deep breath. "Now please talk to me."

He looked down at Valerie who was no more than 5'5 and 150 pounds soaking wet. "It's nothing." He grabbed her hands from his face, kissed them and kissed her cheek. "And I'll be alright, the last thing I need is for you to worry."

He walked out of the house and she went to his window and watched his car pull off. She took a moment to collect her thoughts before walking into the front room. Her husband, Steve sat on the sofa drinking a cup of coffee, while reading the newspaper.

"You still in there bothering that boy?" he sat the coffee down and flipped the page.

"Something ain't right, Steve." There was an emptiness in the pit of her stomach. "I know my son and as sure as I'm standing here I'm telling you that something is wrong."

He slammed the paper on his lap. "Why, because he doesn't run behind his mother anymore? Because he's *growing up and has a life outside of us? Because I keep telling you that I'm your husband. Your son is not, and you have to let him go."*

"Why do you have to be so disgusting? You know what I mean."

He laughed. "What I think is that you don't know when to let go. Whatever Rico is going through he will tell you when it's the right time." He paused. "For all we know it may be that the police arrested his cousin." He picked the paper up again. "Really, try not to worry so much."

She exhaled. "I hope you're right."

RICO – IN SCHOOL

Rico wore shades to school and as he moved through the hallway his head was low. The plan was to finish his classes, avoid lunch and go home. But as he continued down the hall he noticed people were looking at him funny, like they knew something he didn't. At first he thought it was his shades, but when he saw Joanne at his locker, dressed like a boy, he felt gut punched. With kind eyes he said, "I'm sorry, Rico, I just couldn't lie anymore."

178   By Paige Lohan

Rico backed away from Joe and bumped into a few kids who were looking their way, trying to understand how the pretty girl transformed into a pretty boy over night. Devastated and needing to get away, he moved quickly toward the gym. Just five seconds he told himself was all he needed to make sense out of everything. There had to be a way to get his life together, he just needed to figure it all out.

When he got there it was empty and he found himself on the bleachers, up high, away from the floor. He placed his book bag on one of the benches, opened it up and removed the gun that belonged to his father. When he first took it from the house he told himself there wasn't a firm reason, but if he thought harder he'd remember clearly. Last night he planned to kill Joe for his betrayal.

His life would never be the same and he was thinking about what he would do next when Joe walked into the gymnasium, hands tucked inside his pockets. Rico quickly stuffed the gun in his waist and pulled his shirt down before he saw it. "What are you doing here?"

"Are you okay?" Joe asked, his voice soft and low.

"Like you give a fuck."

Joe moved closer. "I know you don't believe me, but I'm so sorry, Rico. I just couldn't play the games anymore."

Rico's eyes were red and glassy. "A game huh? That's all it was to you?"

Joe wiped the tears off his face and sighed, "Of course not! The only thing I wanted in this world was to love you. And I would rather you know the truth about me then to fall deeper than you already had."

As Rico listened, the thing he hated most was that although Joe was a boy, his mannerisms were the same. He talked like his Joanne, moved like his Joanne and now that he was closer, even looked like her minus the makeup and wigs. Still he asked himself why hadn't he known before.

"Why did you have to come to school like this? Why couldn't you wait, and just leave after the school year?" he yelled. "When you go back to North Carolina I still have to live here! Did you ever give a fuck about that?"

Joe looked down and considered what he said. In his plight to do the right thing he gave no thought to how Rico would feel being publicly humiliated. Because it wasn't his plan. He was about to apologize when he looked up and saw Rico pointing a gun in his direction.

"You fucking ruined my life!" Rico yelled, the gun shaking in his hand. He stood up and walked toward him.

Joe placed his hands in the air. "Please don't do this, Rico. You don't want to do this, I'm begging you."

"You ruined everything for me!" He cocked the gun.

Joe's chin quivered. "My mama, my mama would never be able to deal with this. Please don't take me away from her, I'm begging you."

"Why should I give a fuck about her? Huh! You didn't care about me, or my mother."

Joe's body felt heavy and he dropped to his knees. It was all over and there he was again, about to die at a school.

Rico placed the gun to the top of his head and was about to pull the trigger until he looked down. He was still in love. Was it possible that he'd known he was a boy all along but fear caused him to deny the truth? Maybe he wanted Joe to continue with the façade so that he wouldn't have to admit who he really was, a gay boy who would never be able to express himself openly.

"I wish you never came here," he said through tears before turning the gun on himself and pulling the trigger.

CHAPTER SEVENTEEN

JOE

I was hysterical. Blood was all over my clothes from pressing my hand over the wound on Rico's head, from when he blew his brains out.

As I sat in Mrs. Holbrook's car, because my aunt wouldn't answer the phone when they called, my mind swirled with what just happened and I felt weak, my body was in a ball of emotions. What am I going to do? Who will I be after watching a person I loved kill himself, over what I'd done?

"We're here," Mrs. Holbrook said touching my leg. "Are you okay?"

I didn't respond. Words seemed too weak for the moment. I needed something stronger, maybe alcohol, or drugs. Instead I looked over at her, tears running down my cheeks, my heart pumping out of my chest.

"This isn't your fault, honey, although it may seem that way." Her smile was partly full, and I could sense behind it something judgmental, although she was desperately trying to prevent it from showing. "I don't know why you decided not to be who God intended, but it wasn't your fault that boy killed himself."

I wiped the tears away with a rough swat that made my eyes throb. "Then why does it feel like I'm responsible? He cared about me and I betrayed his trust, now he's gone."

Her pressure on my thigh was suddenly a little harder, like she was trying to hurt me while pretending it was affection. "Because you were there, Joe. That's why it feels that way. I don't know what you all talked about before he pulled the trigger. I'll leave it to the police because it isn't my place. I just want to remind you that it wasn't your gun. Give it some time, things will get better."

I hated when people did that sort of thing. Lie to me about the future when the present was too fucked up to make any good opinions. I knew that my life would be anything but better and that the guilt of what happened today would forever stay with me. "Thank you," I said, as I pulled the door to exit. "For the ride too."

Before I left she said, "Why did you want to come here? Instead of to your house?"

"Because I want to be with somebody who feels as badly as I do." I shrugged.

I left the car, closed it softly and walked toward Canyetta's door. Before I knocked she opened it, a ball of tissue paper stuck in her hand. I didn't go inside right away; instead I looked into her eyes, trying to figure out if she hated me like everyone else at school.

After Rico killed himself, police swarmed the gymnasium and everybody who loved him was crying. Lying in the hallways, in the classrooms, it was so sad. I never felt mass pain on that level and I never wanted to again.

"I didn't think you would come," she said, sniffling a little. "After what you just saw."

I shifted and crossed my arms over my chest. "You invited me and I wanted to be anywhere else but home. Is the invitation still open?"

She opened the door wider and I walked inside. Something about her house seemed dark, untrustworthy, but still, it was better than home. In less than two weeks I managed to lose my cousin, my first love and worsen my relationship with my aunt.

By Paige Lohan

"You want something to drink?" she stood in front of me, placing her hands on her hips. She was on the defensive and I realized maybe this was a bad idea.

"You still got that fruity stuff you talked about? Because I could use a drink." I sat on the sofa, legs crossed at the ankles and palms on my knees. Don't know why I picked this awkward position; guess it felt comfortable even though I was no longer in drag.

"I got wine coolers, beer and vodka I think. My mom doesn't keep a lot of food in the house but the cooler stays packed." She tried to smile but it must've felt too heavy because it wiped away.

"You can give me anything."

"A girl after my own heart," she grinned. And then, as if she remembered something she said, "Do you prefer to be called a girl still?"

"I just prefer to be called my name, and it's Joe."

"Fair enough." She walked into the kitchen and I heard the refrigerator open and close. A few minutes later she came back with two large pink plastic cups. She handed one to me and kept the other for herself. I thought she might have poisoned it but I drank it anyway.

"He never really liked me you know," she said, sitting in a chair across from me. "I tried all I could to make him see that I cared about him. That I really loved him and nothing worked." Her brows lowered. "What was it about you that he liked so much?"

"I don't know," I admitted, taking a big gulp. "Nothing about myself at the time was the truth. Everything was a lie." I shook the cup filled with ice out of nervousness. It made too much noise. "I guess you never know what a person wants."

"Maybe that's what it was." Her eyes appeared dark. "Men like to believe what they want, even if it's someone faking like they got a pussy when they don't." She took a sip and sat her cup on the floor.

My eyes widened. "Excuse me."

"You're a fucking liar, Joanne, or Joe," she yelled. "And it's your fault that Rico isn't here anymore. It's your fault that the one person I cared about shot himself in the head!"

I placed the cup down. I could feel the rage pouring out of her. My first intention was to leave but maybe I needed to hear this. Maybe running was getting old and I deserved everything I was about to get.

By Paige Lohan

One Hour Later

Carlo pulled up in front of Canyetta's house, and beeped several times. A few minutes later she walked outside and rushed to the car. "Why you beeping and shit?" she whispered. "Had she been in the living room she would've seen you."

He scratched his nose. "So she in there?"

"Didn't you tell me to bring her?" she was highly irritated. "I did what you asked!"

"What's wrong with you?"

"Fucking Rico is dead, Carlo! People are dying at the school and I didn't sign up for all of this death. That's what's wrong with me."

He nodded. "Yeah, I heard about that." He shook his head. "I can't believe both of them bitches niggas. My man killed himself fucking with a tranny but I got his back." He removed a gun from his waist and cocked it. "He should have did what me and Thomas did."

She eyed the weapon and leaned back. "So what you want me to do?" she looked at him and the gun again.

"Nothing, I got this shit."

"Are you gonna do him like you did Luke, because I heard it was bad."

"Why you worried?" he frowned.

"Because I don't want blood all over my mama's carpet!"

"Naw, I used a knife on that nigga. I ain't got time for that shit today." He tucked the weapon back in his waist. "What time my aunt get home?" he looked at the clock.

"Two hours." She ran her hands down her face. "I slapped him, and we got into a quick fight. A little while ago."

He smiled slyly. "Wait, you hit that bitch?" He rubbed his hands together like he was hearing a good story.

"Yeah, but he acted like he didn't care." She shrugged. "Maybe he feels guilty."

"That bitch not guilty and he don't care either, or he wouldn't have done it." He frowned. "Anyway, I may need you to help me move the body. I wouldn't want my aunt coming home and seeing it."

Her eyes widened. "What, you didn't say I needed to help?"

"Fuck you want me to do, carry it out on my shoulders and throw it in the trunk?"

By Paige Lohan

Canyetta sighed heavily. "I'ma do whatever, just make it quick. Okay?"

After the details were drawn they both stepped out of the car, walking quickly toward the house. Carlo looked around to be sure no one was watching him. Once they were inside Carlo walked up to Joe who stood up when he saw him come inside.

"What are you doing here?" Joe asked, eyes wide.

Carlo laughed. "Don't worry about all that, bitch! What you should be asking is what's getting ready to happen to you." He pulled the gun from his waist.

"Is it true, that you had something to do with killing my cousin?" Joe was stiff as a board.

"What the fuck do you think? I had everything to do with it."

He was just about to fire when five police officers poured out of the back rooms. One of them, a large white man with an angry face was the first to reach Carlo. With a swift hit to the neck with a forearm he knocked him down and the gun was taken away.

Carlo coughed a few times, confused as to what was going on. When his breathing was under control he looked up at Canyetta as the cops checked him for more weapons. "You stupid, bitch! I should've known I couldn't trust you!"

"I'm not with this kind of shit, Carlo," Canyetta cried. "I ain't with none of it."

Carlo was lifted to his feet and dragged out of the door.

By Paige Lohan

CHAPTER EIGHTEEN

TWO YEARS LATER

JOE

I never knew New York could be like this! I heard about the culture but it wasn't until I moved here one year ago that I really fell in love.

After making a pot of beef and broccoli soup, I scooped some and put it over rice, using my red bowls. Carefully I walked to the top of my brownstone, where my mother stayed. She moved in with me six months ago after the constant death threats she received almost three years after the incident at my North Carolina high school. After all that time the people didn't want to let it go and couldn't rest with her living there.

The best thing about all of this was that my mother's cancer was in remission. With Luke dead I got the feeling she was trying to stay alive for me.

My mother was sitting on the edge of the bed, looking at TV. "Here you go, mama," I placed the tray on her lap. "Anything else?"

"No, just sit down with me," she said patting the bed. "It won't take but a moment."

I took a seat, grabbed the remote and turned down the TV. "Are you okay?" I touched her hand and she smiled. "Because you look better."

"I'm perfect, but sometimes I worry about you, Joe. Something feels wrong and I don't know what it is. Tell me I'm being silly so I can let it go."

Mother always worried even though I had proven that I was grown and could take care of myself. When the money from my lawsuit came the first thing I did was buy this brownstone. I also bought a better headstone for Rico and started a college fund in his name. His mother and father never forgave me but I didn't expect them to.

Carlo and Thomas were convicted for my cousin's death, tried as adults and given life sentences. There were a lot of people who claimed they were warranted for killing Luke since he lied about who he was. But I decided not to worry about that kind of stuff anymore. If they felt that way, that was their opinions.

No matter how happy I was my mother always believed there was something else hiding behind my eyes. "Mama, I don't know what you want me to say. I

By Paige Lohan

have come to terms with what happened to Rico and Luke. The only thing I want to do now is live my life."

She placed the tray on the bed and positioned her body so that she was looking at me. She grabbed both of my hands. "Have you forgiven Stacy?"

I frowned, stood up and walked toward the corner of her room. "I can't do that right now, mama." I crossed my arms over my chest. "And it's wrong for you to ask me that. We all have to grieve how we need to and right now I don't want to talk to her."

She sighed. "Joe, there will come a time when you will want forgiveness. I only hope you feel the same way you do now." She smiled, took a deep breath and clapped her hands together once. "Well, let me eat." Picking up the tray again she took a bite. "Wow, this is good. Really good."

"I knew it would be," I smiled. "It's your recipe."

"Thief." She winked. "So how long is your drive?"

"A few hours but I'm staying overnight."

"And where you going again?"

"To see my friend Canyetta I was telling you about." I kissed her on the forehead. "But I really do have to go, mama. My friend Karen next door is going to check on you. If you need anything just call her. The number is on the refrigerator."

"I keep telling you, you don't have to do that. I'm walking and everything now."

"I know, but one of the reasons you're doing so well is because you rest. There will be plenty of time for you to run around New York."

"I guess I can't argue with you."

After my mother was taken care of I jumped in my new silver Cadillac Escalade and took the long drive down south. I hated lying to my mother but the last person on earth I was going to see was Canyetta. We weren't friends in high school and we weren't cool now. Especially since she didn't tell the cops when she agreed to wear a wire that Carlo had a gun the day he was supposed to kill me. Had they known that, they would've knocked him down the moment he came through the door, instead of getting his confession.

I was surprised when I came to the house that day only to realize she needed me to help the cops because her cousin was about to kill me. Although in court she said she couldn't see another person die I know the real reason she helped was because she didn't want to get in trouble. She ended up cooperating with the police and told them everything they needed to know.

In exchange for her testimony she was given immunity after learning that they set my cousin up with the fake party, only for him to be killed. I wanted them all to burn but at least Carlo and Thomas went down.

Nine hours later I was at my destination. I popped the glove compartment and removed my .45. Once I cocked it I looked across the large field. It was crowded with other players but I knew his body even with the helmet.

I placed a hoodie over my head, pulled the drawstrings and rushed toward him. The North Carolina trip was long but I would make sure it was well worth it.

When I got up on Marcus I placed the gun to his back, his teammates ran, I guess they saw the gun before he did. By the time he turned around the gun was aimed at him. "Please don't," he pleaded, his hands in the air. He wasn't so bad anymore.

"My cousin said the same thing before you almost killed him. So did I." I shot him three times in the chest and once in his groin. "That was for Luke." I dropped the gun on him and ran quickly toward my truck.

I was changed now. The only thing is I'm not sure if it was for the better or worse.

By Paige Lohan

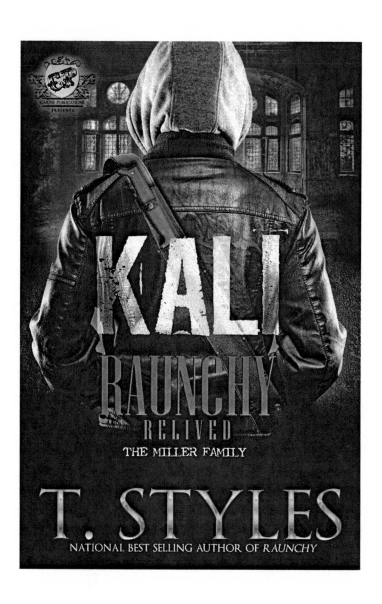

KALI
RAUNCHY
RELIVED

THE MILLER FAMILY

T. STYLES

NATIONAL BEST SELLING AUTHOR OF *RAUNCHY*

The Cartel Publications Order Form
www.thecartelpublications.com
Inmates **ONLY** receive novels for $10.00 per book.
(Mail Order **MUST** come from inmate directly to receive discount)

Shyt List 1	_____	$15.00
Shyt List 2	_____	$15.00
Shyt List 3	_____	$15.00
Shyt List 4	_____	$15.00
Shyt List 5	_____	$15.00
Pitbulls In A Skirt	_____	$15.00
Pitbulls In A Skirt 2	_____	$15.00
Pitbulls In A Skirt 3	_____	$15.00
Pitbulls In A Skirt 4	_____	$15.00
Victoria's Secret	_____	$15.00
Poison 1	_____	$15.00
Poison 2	_____	$15.00
Hell Razor Honeys	_____	$15.00
Hell Razor Honeys 2	_____	$15.00
A Hustler's Son 2	_____	$15.00
Black and Ugly As Ever	_____	$15.00
Year Of The Crackmom	_____	$15.00
Deadheads	_____	$15.00
The Face That Launched A	_____	$15.00
Thousand Bullets		
The Unusual Suspects	_____	$15.00
Miss Wayne & The Queens of DC	_____	$15.00
Paid In Blood (eBook Only)	_____	$15.00
Raunchy	_____	$15.00
Raunchy 2	_____	$15.00
Raunchy 3	_____	$15.00
Mad Maxxx	_____	$15.00
Quita's Dayscare Center	_____	$15.00
Quita's Dayscare Center 2	_____	$15.00
Pretty Kings	_____	$15.00
Pretty Kings 2	_____	$15.00
Pretty Kings 3	_____	$15.00
Silence Of The Nine	_____	$15.00
Silence Of The Nine 2	_____	$15.00
Prison Throne	_____	$15.00
Drunk & Hot Girls	_____	$15.00
Hersband Material	_____	$15.00
The End: How To Write A	_____	$15.00
Bestselling Novel In 30 Days (Non-Fiction Guide)		
Upscale Kittens	_____	$15.00

By Paige Lohan

Wake & Bake Boys	_____	$15.00
Young & Dumb	_____	$15.00
Young & Dumb 2:	_____	$15.00
Tranny 911	_____	$15.00
Tranny 911: Dixie's Rise	_____	$15.00
First Comes Love, Then Comes Murder	_____	$15.00
Luxury Tax	_____	$15.00
The Lying King	_____	$15.00
Crazy Kind Of Love	_____	$15.00
And They Call Me God	_____	$15.00
The Ungrateful Bastards	_____	$15.00
Lipstick Dom	_____	$15.00
A School of Dolls	_____	$15.00

Please add $4.00 **PER BOOK** for shipping and handling.

The Cartel Publications * P.O. BOX 486 OWINGS MILLS MD 21117

Name: _____

Address: _____

City/State: _____

Contact# & Email:

_____

Please allow 5-7 BUSINESS days before shipping.

The Cartel Publications is NOT responsible for prison orders rejected.

NO PERSONAL CHECKS ACCEPTED

STAMPS NO LONGER ACCEPTED